Cows

AKCHARA MUKUNTHU

ISBN: 9798338149010

DEDICATION

To my family and friends – people and animals. Especially

my grandmother, Pavalam, who is a pillar of support and

kindness in my life - thank you for everything!

COWS

CONTENTS

Acknowledgments

Foreword

Introduction

About the Author

COWS

COWS

COWS

ACKNOWLEDGMENTS

Special appreciation to my parents who always encourage me in my writing. They helped review this book and provided crucial feedback throughout the process.

Also, thank you to my sister for being there for me and making me laugh when I need it most.

COWS

FOREWORD

Since Akchara's childhood, I have known her because I am her grandmother, and I raised her. Every day we would go on walks together and whenever she would see the animals, she would pause. Around her, she would admire the sights of the parrots, dogs, sheep, and more. She would pet them and feed them.

Even to this day, she is an aquatic hobbyist who maintains two fish tanks. She feeds her fish every morning before school. She tries to engage in animal advocacy whenever she can. She is compassionate to not only all humans but animals, too. She always spends her time researching about them to know more. When she approached me about this idea for her new book *Cows,* I was very touched that she is writing about this important, animal-related topic. I always read her articles on *Medium* and give her feedback. Even though my English is not great, I try to support my granddaughter in her writing endeavors. I am extremely proud of Akchara's talents including her writing and proud to call her my granddaughter.

INTRODUCTION

I authored this book, *Cows*, with three main purposes. I want to educate you all (readers) about animal rights, entertain students through a fun story, and show a glimpse of the realistic life of a girl in India.

Nikitha's life is vastly different from someone's life in a first-world country. Many times, we don't realize how privileged we are but by exposing readers to Nikitha's struggles, I want them to realize that.

Some of the luxuries we have gotten used to, like eating at restaurants and watching movies are way out of reach for people like Nikitha. They are more concerned about having food on the table and attending school.

In the process of reading this book, I want you to question yourself this: "Do I ever take what I have granted? How can I help my community like Nikitha is trying to do?"

Those questions are enough to encourage thought-provoking behavior and powerful actions.

Animal rights issues are becoming far too cliché, so I chose a particular issue which is not generic but relevant to the current day and age.

This story takes place in Palakkad, a city on the border of the states, Kerala, and Tamil Nadu, in India. It is a breezy, jolly story which explores all aspects of life: the sweet and bitter.

Originally, I was inspired to write this book on a road trip with my family where I saw a pen of cows just like in this story. I was heartbroken and knew I had to do something like Nikku did. That is why I am spreading awareness through *Cows*. Besides that, I love meeting cows in village settings like I was able to do at a temple in India and here, too.

I wrote it from the point of view of a child main character to be more relatable and empower my audience to create change in their own lives. Age is just a number which does not define what we can and cannot do. If you want to save the world and inspire change, you can do it.

COWS

CHAPTER 1
HELLO, WORLD!

"Ma, I'm home!" I exclaim, running into our straw hut.

This hut, with how low it is, is one of many things that annoys my mother. She constantly must bend to come inside, and it gives her back pain. If only the hut was taller or Ma was shorter, then it would be more comfortable for use. She strains her body all day long what with her job as a washerwoman, so I feel bad that she exhausts herself at home too. I wish there were something I could do!

My teacher, Latha Madam, used to tell us about contraptions in the city like the washing machine. She said that it is like a robot that people invented to replace washing by hand. A part of me wishes that Ma had a washing machine so that she would not need to wash all the villagers' clothes by hand. But her entire livelihood is based off washing by hand and our family would not have any money if it were not for that.

Ma is a washerwoman because she followed the footsteps of her mother and grandmother. That is simply a polished way of saying it. The truth is that she was forced to due to her family lifestyle. It is generational and has been passed down like jewelry and stories.

However, she definitely does not want me to become like her when I grow up. Washing clothes is all she knows. If only she had studied, then she would be able to easily pick up a new job. I guess good thing that there are no washing machines since they would take away from my family's source of income, washing by hand.

Forget washing machines, there are lots of other machines that would be useful for us like a fridge or a grinder. The coolest one in my opinion is the phone. In our village, if you need to contact someone, you need to pass the message on to someone else or talk with them in person. An epic waste of time and energy! With a phone, we could contact anyone at the press of a button.

The only reason households in our village cannot have these amazing inventions is because of the cost. If someone goes to the trouble of inventing these trinkets, they should go a step further to make sure it is accessible for all. I understand that they would need to lower the price for the villagers and would make less profits, but it would make our lives much easier. Rich people never seem to consider the villagers and their quality of life.

Families from our village have been farming for years and years – providing the world with crops to eat. Every grain of rice, every bit of sugar, every piece of fresh produce that the world consumes is due to the arduous work that farmers and their families put in. Rain or shine, the farmers go out to the plantations and work. I have seen them wipe layers of sweat off their foreheads and get badly sunburned as they plow through hard days. They don't even get paid that much at all for their toil!

You might say it is their fault for not studying well in school but often, their families withdraw them from schooling at a young age. They never had a choice about how much effort they put into school because that opportunity was taken from them. Due to generational poverty, many children don't get the chance to study and are forced to do strenuous work like farming to make a living.

"Shh, Nikku, be quiet! I just put Kanna to sleep," Ma whisper-shouts.

My name is Nikitha, but my close family and friends call me Nikku — my parents came up with the pet name. They felt like my cute baby face deserved a different name and Nikku was perfect. Sometimes, I even forget my real name.

Kanna is my little brother. He is very mischievous like the real Kanna, Lord Krishna, was as a child. He can be kind of a pain at times, but Ma tells me to wait until he grows up. Apparently, then he will become a great friend to me. I am being patient but if the waiting is not worth it – I swear I am going to go ballistic!

"Sorry, Ma. I didn't know," I apologize.

"It's okay," she glances outside, "Oh my, it has gotten dark. Why are you so late?"

"Oh, my bad. We were deep into a game of jacks, and I was about to win so I stayed out longer and did you know, in the end it was..."

Ma interrupts, "I don't want to know the details. Bottom line is you must come back home before sundown. That was our deal, remember?"

"Yes, Ma!" I groan.

"Listen, I could just have you stay at home all day while I work. The only reason I am letting you wander around the village is, so you're not bored. This is a privilege which I can take away," she sighs and pauses, "Look me in the eyes and promise."

"I promise this will never happen again. Hey, wait a minute...you have bags under your eyes again. Did you sleep last night?" I ask.

I usually leave at dawn to roam. All my friends who live in the neighborhood are at school, so I just go around doing random things. I could leave later if I wanted to, but it is nice at dawn where there are barely any vehicles, and you can be one with nature.

When I leave home, Ma and Kanna are still in bed, so I don't get to check on them until the evening after my mother returns from her job. I am forced to assume that Ma is sleeping but I know that is far from the truth.

"Not really. I have not been able to sleep at all," she replies.

This is the same thing she has told me for days now. I am worried about her health. Doctor Uncle told us the other day that sleep is the best medicine and without it, the body slowly shuts down. I keep reminding Ma but what can she do? Sleep is not in our control. She never mentions why she cannot sleep but I know. One event changed everything.

CHAPTER 2
PA

I remember it vividly. It was just a normal afternoon. I had gotten home from school and was doing my homework in the bedroom while Ma was cutting vegetables in the kitchen. I felt an eerie sense of calm right before disaster strikes. I shuddered with chills on my back.

Right then, an old lady walked to our door, holding her hip. She looked exhausted and was out of breath. It seemed like she had walked fast to get to our house. I did not know her that well but recognized her as one of the elders of the Panchayat. They are the five respected elders of the village that make the decisions -

kind of like the members of government. Upon seeing her, Ma carefully stood up.

"Oh, Ambika Aunty, please come in. Would you like some tea or coffee? Yesterday, at the market, I found some fresh mangoes and guavas..."

"No, no, I don't want anything. Kamla, I know this might be hard to hear, dear..." she paused.

"What is it? Please tell me," Ma urged her.

"Oh, dear gods, your family is precious as gold, I don't know why this happened to you guys," she said, her head hung down.

"What do you mean? We are completely fine," Ma replied, oblivious.

"Ah, you see, I was just near the bank. Your husband...was found with the police...he was arrested," she spitted out.

Ma took time to process the news and then her face changed. She looked shocked, confused, and scared. She was in complete disbelief. I, on the other hand, was panicking. Someone going to prison is certainly not something that happens on a daily basis. Next to our village, there is an old prison in town. I have heard horror stories of the cruel punishments and forms of torture they use there. I winced thinking about all of that and especially Pa facing it. He would not even hurt a fly, so I wondered why they arrested him. Ma did too.

"That is not possible, Aunty. I know him, he would not do anything bad. We have been married for years and I trust him with my whole heart. I think there is a mix-up here," Ma told her.

The lady asked her, "He didn't do anything bad, but he was still arrested. Your husband's name is Krishnan, no?"

She nodded and sniffled, "Yes, what happened?"

The lady hesitated at first but proceeded to tell us the entire story. Apparently, Pa was coming back home but stopped in front of the bank. Someone screamed for help, so he rushed in to see what it was.

As it turns out, the bank had been hijacked by a group of criminals that day. The person who Pa followed in was one of them acting. They had stolen all the money from the safe and tied up the employees. They needed to find some innocent villager to be the scapegoat and take the blame for the crime which they did not commit.

Unfortunately, it was Pa's fate that he became that guy. He walked in as they made their escape. He was probably clueless but when the police found him at the scene of the crime as the only person not tied up, he looked like a culprit. I wish I were there with him so I could have told the police that my father is innocent. They wouldn't have believed me anyway though as I am just a little girl.

Ma asked the old lady, "But if he was not guilty, why didn't he say something? Why did the police arrest him?"

"I don't know, sorry, dear. As soon as I heard, I

came here. A group of men from our village went to the police station and sent me here to inform you. I would suggest you go there and inquire."

"Ma, can I come please? I have always wanted to know what a police station is like!" I exclaimed, unaware of the seriousness of the situation.

"No, Nikku. This is a job for Ma to do alone. Grandma can stay home with you," she said in a kind tone, referring to the old lady.

"Ma, I want to see if Pa is okay!" I cried.

She put her hands on my face – one hand on each cheek – and assured, "He will be fine. I am sure of it."

Ma is a great matriarch. The way her voice uttered those words, full of confidence, even though she had no idea about Pa's state gave me a boost of belief. Little did I know that it was false hope. She came home a while later, sobbing.

I ran to her and asked, "Ma, what happened?

Why are you crying? Is Pa okay?"

She wiped away her tears and got ready to speak to me in a motherly tone.

"It looks like you and I can spend some time together for a while, Nikku."

"What do you mean?" I ask, bewildered.

She gestures to her pregnant belly, "When I give birth, you will need to help in raising and caring for your sibling. I think the two of us – strong women – can handle the job."

The young child I was back then did not understand what was going on. Ma just indirectly told me that we would have to be without Pa. I didn't get it. I wish I had understood earlier, though.

"So, when is Pa coming home?" I asked, clueless.

Ma sighed and did not say anything. Instead, she simply walked into the kitchen. She couldn't bear to tell me that he wasn't coming back and break my heart. She thought the silence was obvious. But not for me. I waited every day with the hope that he would return.

One day, I was playing in the sand pit at school and some mean boys walked over and yelled, "Nickle, your father is in jail! He is not coming back!"

Those jerks always call me 'Nickle' to bug me and try to irritate me. They would say that is my metaphorical worth. I thought this was another trick and didn't believe them when they said Pa would not return.

If you are surprised how they know about Pa, in my small village, every news spreads like wildfire. Eventually, everyone including the kids finds out.

"Well, if that is the case, then why did my mother not tell me straight-up?" I ask.

"She just doesn't want you to be sad, but we think you deserve to know the truth," one boy sneered.

I could tell they just wanted to ruin my spirit. As they say, ignorance is bliss. If I had not found out that early, the hope that Pa might come would have kept me going. That same day, I came home upset.

"Ma! Why did you not tell me that Pa is not coming back? The boys at my school told me today!" I screamed.

She looked at me with sad eyes. And once again, said nothing. Sometimes I feel angry that my mom is quiet when she has to say something, anything.

Pa's arrest was extremely hard on Ma. It could not have been at a worse time. She was pregnant with Kanna, and our family was just getting by. Since pregnant women should not exhaust themselves too much, she could not even do her job as a washerwoman. Some days she didn't even want to get out of bed. She would have been cooped up in our room all the time if not for me. I consoled her, telling her that things would get better soon.

My moral support made Ma feel better for a while until she thought of reality. We didn't have enough money without Pa's salary. We had to do something to gather the funds. We had no choice but to go into debt. Ma's family is completely against it, so she was raised being taught to avoid it, but it was our only hope. Even to this day, three years later, Ma is still working, bit by bit, to pay off the debts and loans.

As a last resort, right before going into debt, she tried asking relatives for help, but no one would answer her calls or let her into their houses. This is because Ma and Pa fell in love and got married against their families' wishes. We are now shunned from both sides of the family. I finally understand why I never had a grandma to hug, a grandpa to tell me stories, an uncle to buy me gifts, an aunt to cook my favorite foods, or cousins to play with. It was always just my parents and me.

Of course, the most important cause was to bail Pa out of prison. Ma went to many trials at the court, but nothing worked. She knew the reason was because the free legal aid facility's lawyers were all bad quality.

Since they could not get hired at any proper law firm, they worked for the government and barely tried to do their jobs. There was no need for them to work properly because they rarely got clients. Again, a roadblock for poor people.

Knowing Pa would not get out of prison anytime soon was devastating for both of us. I know you are thinking that we can just visit Pa to feel better. But it is not so.

Ma went once a few weeks after his arrest. She was normal when she left home but came back crying. She could not bear seeing him behind bars like a caged animal. Miserable. After that incident, she never went near the jail again and I was not allowed to either. I considered sneaking in so I could see Pa, but I needed an adult to accompany me, and I knew of no adults that would help.

One time, I came home from school and Ma was nowhere to be seen. I finally found her in bed. I spied on her from a distance. She was holding a photo of Pa with her hand over his face, wiping the tears pouring out of her eyes.

"Krishna! Krishna! Come back!" she wailed.

I could not stand seeing her sorrow. I had only seen this happen once but imagine, how many times has Ma been alone pondering about Pa, uttering his name with the chance that maybe, maybe he hears?

How could I ever forget Pa? His sweet face, gentle eyes, and laugh – oh, his laugh! Latha Madam once told us about Santa Claus. He is an old man with a big white beard who would let out deep laughs as he gave gifts to the children of the world. Pa laughed just like him. Unfortunately, I don't think he has laughed in a long time.

But a part of me thinks, what if he has decided to forget us since he does not know if we will ever get reunited? The thought of him laughing and having good times with other people and telling jokes to other little kids stings. Pa called my mom and I, his life. What if someone else takes that place in his heart? I feel myself becoming delusional but who knows what is happening in his life right now?

CHAPTER 3
OUR STRUGGLES

Before, Ma always had a big smile plastered across her face. Nowadays, it just feels like all the joy faded from her life. She has apologized so many times for our unfortunate lives and is trying her best not to affect us too much. Sometimes she doesn't have enough money to cook for all of us. She has starved so we don't go hungry. All this sacrifice and stress is too much for her. She needs to understand that at some point her body will break down, unable to take it. Maybe it is breaking down right now.

"Do you need to consult with a doctor?" I ask, already knowing she will say no.

She shakes her head. I can tell she wants to, but we are running tight on money and cannot afford to spend. To pay medical bills, we would have to get another loan which we now know is torture.

"Worry about yourself, dear. I will be fine. There was something else I wanted to tell you...," she thinks, "Oh, yeah. I have some amazing news for you!"

I put on a puzzled look. The only news that can make me happy now is if it is that Pa has been released. That would fill me with rays of sunshine enough to light the universe.

"What is it?" I ask, curiously.

"Well, I know how sad you have been that you cannot go to school anymore since we cannot afford it but there is this opportunity that I thought you would like to hear. Kaveer's mother, Shami Aunty, offered to be your personal tutor. You can go to school at their house. It is way more useful than wandering around the village. Are you interested?" Ma asks.

I am furious at Ma right now! I absolutely despise Kaveer. He has been out to get me since we were little. Apparently, one time when we were babies, he pulled my hair or at least the few hairs I had back then. I don't know why he dislikes me that much. It is not like I did anything to him. Every time he looks at me, there is a frown on his face. From time to time, there is a slight smile that feels welcoming but often things that seem too good to be true are not true. Usually, that smile indicates danger from him is coming my way. He has set up many pranks to get on my nerves.

Whenever I complain about him to Ma, she grins and says, "It is all fun among you children. Don't take it to heart."

"Ma, you know I hate Kaveer!" I cry.

"Now, Nikku, you must not express hatred towards anyone. Shami Aunty has graciously offered up this opportunity for you. She has a big heart that she is doing this free of charge when she can do many things with her life. Her time is valuable, and she is choosing to use it on you. She told me about how important education is. In the future, I want you to be as successful as your friends that are in school. Don't you?" she asks.

"Yes, but I wish I could go to real school where I can meet my friends and teachers."

"I do too but this is what we have at this point. We need to make do. Soon enough, after I have paid off all the loans and we are stable, I will think about sending you to school. I have been thinking about the future for you and Kanna. I need to start saving up for your weddings," she explains.

"What? Already? But we are just children!"

"I know, I know. But weddings are expensive and with the rate I am earning, it will be wise to start saving early," she replies, "Think it over and let me know. I will tell her. She said you can get started right away."

I don't want to sound ungrateful so I tell her, "Ma, I will try it out. I think I'm going to like it."

"That's the spirit! Tomorrow will be your first day. You must be up and ready in the morning. Now it is time to sleep," she reminds me.

"What about dinner?" I ask.

"Oh, shoot, I was so tired I forgot to make it, and we ran out of food. What do we do?"

Her sleep deprivation is so bad she forgot to cook dinner? This has never happened before and increases my worry about her. I take some time to think of what to say.

"That's okay. We can just go to bed now. I am not that hungry anyway," I lie.

I don't want Ma to feel bad that I am going to sleep hungry but do wish that we had some food.

"Are you sure? I can go to the shop to buy something," she suggests.

I would love that, but it will be expensive, and

spending is Ma's worst fear. It will just make her sleep less. I have heard her sleep-talk at night and say things about how much we are spending and how little money we have right now. I must pretend to be satisfied and not want any food for my mother's sake.

"No, there is no need for that. The lentils and rice you made for lunch were really filling. Thanks, Ma," I exclaim as I hug her.

She is startled but replies, "Okay, that's great. Now go to the bedroom and sleep."

Most people think that huts are just a single room, and they usually are but Pa built ours with a kitchen and bedroom. His expertise as a civil engineer helped to design a modern hut with low expense. The outhouse next to the hut is the bathroom. It can be a little crammed at times since it is a small space, but it is cozy. We make do by doubling the kitchen as a dining room and the bedroom as a living room.

I walk into the bedroom and see little Kanna

drawing on a notepad. I sit next to him and look at it.

"Hi, Nikku. Look at what I'm drawing!" he exclaims.

"I see, Kanna. That is such a beautiful...lion?" I guess.

"No, silly, it's a golden tree."

"Really?"

"Yeah, duh. This is the trunk, these are the roots, this is the top with the branches, and these are the leaves," he explains, pointing out each part.

"Oh, okay, now I sort of see it. Well, put it away, time for bed."

"Alright," he sets the notepad off to the side.

I glance outside where Ma is sitting in front of our hut, probably thinking about Pa. She does this every night, and I usually put Kanna to sleep and wait a bit for her to come. She insists I should sleep without her, but I have the fear she might stay out there all night long, worrying.

By and by, I walk over to the fire lamp hanging at the top of the hut and turn it off. Pa installed it when he built this hut. I have gone to my friends' huts, and they are not nearly as sophisticated as ours. I feel lucky, but it would be much more fortunate if Pa were here with us.

In the dark, I struggle but eventually find my way back to the carpet and lie down on my pillow. I rest but stay awake, waiting for Ma to come back inside and sleep. Until then, I decide to play our usual game with Kanna. A long while ago, when Ma started waiting outside the hut, Kanna was not able to sleep so I invented this game to help him. Partly, to help myself, too.

Basically, the game is called guessing game. It can be played with as many people as you want but usually it is just Kanna and I. You play it by having one player think of a random person. It can be anyone as long as everyone playing knows that person. Then, the other players ask questions about that person. The catch is the questions must be able to be answered with just a yes or no. They cannot require any complex answer, sentences, or strings of words. The player thinking of the person answers the questions and the other players try to guess who they are thinking of. It is really entertaining!

"I can't sleep, Nikku. Can we play guessing game?" Kanna asks me right as I am about to ask him the same question.

I knew he would ask that, "Okay, fine. You can think of someone. Let me know when you are ready."

A few moments later, Kanna states, "Yes, I'm ready. Ask questions."

I go on to ask questions about their gender, age, how we know them, and more. Eventually, I correctly guess that it is Arithjai, Kanna's friend who lives a couple huts down.

A long while later, Ma walks in and heads to the

kitchen. I hear the metal clanging and know she is washing the dishes and putting them away. She is so disciplined that she does not ever go to bed without doing this no matter how tired she is. On top of this, instead of just leaving the vessels lying there, she must put the pots and pans in their respective places. She wipes the ground stove top clean and turns off the oil lamp in the kitchen.

She walks to the bedroom and lies down on the other side of Kanna.

"Nikku, dear, are you awake?" she whispers.

"Yes, Ma," I mumble.

To be honest, I was feeling exhausted, but I tried not to show it in my voice.

"I just wanted to say thank you for being so helpful and adjusting with all the changes in our lives. I am sorry for you having to quit school, our struggles, and Pa," she chokes up, "And the thing with Shami Aunty is hopefully good enough for now but I am trying hard for you to be able to go to school. There is just so much going on and..." she sighs in pure exhaustion.

"Ma, Ma, calm down. It's okay. I am totally fine with this. We can work through any obstacle together."

"Ah, it is good to hear you say that, my dear. Good night, sweet dreams."

"Good night, Ma."

A few moments later, she starts speaking again, "One more thing, Nikku."

"Yeah?"

"I love you so much."

"I love you too, Ma. Sleep well."

CHAPTER 4
FIRST DAY AT "SCHOOL"

In the morning, I wake up early and get ready for "school". It seems weird to think of it like that but technically I am going to meet my new teacher, so it is school. Ma tells me to sleep in until 9 AM so I can be fresh and ready to learn.

I usually grab a banana from the kitchen or the tea shop for breakfast. I know it doesn't seem like much, but I don't have huge appetite, so it lasts me till lunch. Today Ma insists on making me a proper breakfast, crispy dosas (lentil crepes) with chutney (spicy sauce). Her reasoning is that breakfast is the most important meal of the day, and it will help me focus on class.

Again, I am concerned about how much it will cost but I don't complain. The dosas tasted scrumptious and I was starving after not eating dinner last night. Besides, bananas can get boring - I'm not a monkey.

I wake up, brush my teeth and shower. Ma wants to pick out my clothes, so I look nice. Everyone knows we are poor, but she says I should dress decently in front of my teacher. She spots small holes and rips in most all my clothing. They are faded and look old, too. We finally settle on a yellow tank top that has a sun on it. I don't wear it much, so it doesn't look too bad. I pair it with my blue cotton shorts. After I get dressed, Ma steps back and takes a good look at me. She approves and we head outside. I convince Ma to let me walk there myself since I know the route, but I can tell she wants to drop me off. I just don't want to waste her time and energy for this, and she agrees.

As I leave, Ma says, "Okay, study well. Remember I know you can do anything, and I believe in you wholeheartedly. Please be respectful to Shami Aunty as she is your teacher after all."

"Yes, Ma, bye!" I wave as I run to Kaveer's house.

They live on the side of our village that is modernized. Their mansion is enormous, and everything is plain white. I think it is supposed to look stylish and cool but to me it looks like a canvas waiting to be painted. In fact, before Kanna was born and Pa was with us, they invited the whole village.

My parents were eating and I left to explore. I opened a door and found the storage closet. For some reason, it had paints of distinct colors. If everything in and outside of the house is white, why would they need colorful paint? One can only wonder.

I took a large can of red paint, opened it up, and went to the nearest white wall. This was away from where the adults were sitting. Then, in one go, I dumped the whole can all over the wall, attempting to make a masterpiece. I set the paint can down to admire it.

Then, my foot accidentally hit the can, and it fell with a bang. Paint was pouring out and flowing like a river. The sound startled the adults, and they dashed to see what the matter was. Shami Aunty rushed so fast that she accidentally slipped on the paint, and it stained her new clothing. Upon first glance, the aunties shrieked.

Ma was so mad at me. You should have seen the death glare she gave me. Pa found the whole thing amusing. He was laughing his head off. The humor of the situation is what he noticed over the costs they would need to pay.

"Krishna, why are you not taking this seriously? *Your* daughter ruined their house and Shami's clothes!" Ma reminded.

Pa clarified, "She is *our* daughter and could be an artist in the future."

I loved his positive outlook on everything. Of course, whenever he made comments like that, it really ticked off Ma.

She would constantly chide, "You are not understanding the seriousness of this situation, Krishna."

He would reply, "Calm down, Kamla. It is not the end of the world."

Right now, I am standing in front of the tall white gates of their place. The watchman looks me straight in the eye. He is quite intimidating with his height and muscular build. On the balcony, I see Shami Aunty wearing hot pink coolers and a neon green visor along with her usual face full of makeup. I bet you could notice her in outer space.

She waves and yells, "Watchman, let the child in!"

The watchman nods and opens the gate for me. His job seems so miserable just having to stand outside Kaveer's house all day. I wonder if he even gets time to eat a proper lunch and take care of himself.

As I walk inside, I take my sandals off at the

entrance. I just bought these sandals recently. Still, they are dirty and crusty compared to the racks and racks of shoes at their house. They are all designer, high-quality, clean shoes. This is just the entrance, there are probably way more inside the house. I bet it is someone's job to make all the shoes look so shiny and polished. What a pitiful job.

I set my slippers aside and walk to the giant double doors. They are painted gold and silver - so beautiful. Just by looking at it, you can tell whoever living inside is rich. That is probably why Kaveer's family chose it. They are the type of rich people that want the whole world to know they are rich like it is no secret.

I see a gold doorbell to my left. I press it and wait.

"The door is open. Come right in," Shami Aunty yells from upstairs.

That's odd. Have they never heard of locking the

door for security? Then I remember that they have guards in front of the gates so bad guys cannot get in. Although you can never be too sure since someone can climb over the walls surrounding their property or sneak in other ways.

I run up the stairs to meet Shami Aunty and start learning. I expect her to be ready with books, a whiteboard, or something a teacher would have to help their student learn. Instead, I find her sitting lazily on the fancy recliner sofa, her legs stretched out. On the television, I notice she is watching the soap opera, *Priya's Home.* I am quite aware of the show since all the aunties watch it, including Ma sometimes when she visits friends who have TVs.

The plot is typical for a TV serial. It is about a girl named Priya who gets kicked out of her family and must find a home of her own. Of course, it is spiced up from her romance with the builder and how her family reacts to her gutsy behavior.

As I walk in, Shami Aunty doesn't pay me any attention or even look at me. I decide to wait patiently and not interrupt her. A few minutes later, the advertisements come on.

That is when she greets me, "Why, hello, Nikitha. So good to see you, dear. Sorry, I was intensely watching *Priya's Home* as it is the season finale."

"No problem, Aunty."

"No, no. From today I am your teacher not your auntie. Call me Ms. Shami."

"Okay, Ms. Shami," I chuckle, awkwardly.

It feels weird to call her anything other than Shami Aunty. That is what I have been calling her since I was little. On the other hand, at school, I called my teachers their name followed by 'madam' if they were female and 'sir' if they were male like Sasha Madam and Yagnish Sir. Shami Madam feels way more comfortable than Ms. Shami but I guess it is her choice.

"That's better! Now today we will be working in

the guest room. Follow me."

I follow her to the room which is accessible from the TV area.

"Okay, prepare to be amazed. This was formerly the guest room, but it has been transformed into your classroom," she opens the door and exclaims, "Tada!"

I am blown away. The room is so colorful, and all the walls are covered in educational posters and artwork. In the side of the room there is a whiteboard with a teacher's desk in front of it. A lone student desk is in the center of the room. There are books stacked on shelves and a fluffy beanbag chair in the corner. It looks like a western classroom which I have only seen in movies and TV. I stay silent for a few moments, admiring its beauty.

"Do you like it?" she asks, breaking the silence.

"Yes, I love it. This is so great! How did you do it?" I ask.

"Oh, haha, *I* didn't do it. We hired some interior

decorators and simply gave them our ideas. They made the magic!"

I suddenly feel guilty. Shami Aunty probably paid a lot for this room. For me. I don't deserve it. A guest room is a much better use of the space. I decide to be honest with her and express my concerns.

"But this is unnecessary. What will you use the room for after my lessons are over or when I go back to school?"

Shami Aunty tutoring me wasn't going to be forever. I knew that much for sure.

"Don't you worry about that, sweetie. Depending on how this goes, I might start a tuition service or change this into a group class sort of thing. I really don't know but teaching children has always been my dream!" she squeals like a little girl.

She walks over to sit behind the teacher desk, and I take my place at the student desk. It certainly feels weird to be in this setup as the only student. Shami

Aunty then heads over to the bookshelf to grab some books for me.

She sets two second-grade books on my desk and says, "Here you go. These are yours now."

I am confused. Surely, she must know I am Kaveer's age and should be in fifth grade. I remember working in these books before Pa was arrested - back when I went to school. Also, I notice the covers have Kaveer's name on them and assume the insides are all written in. Second-hand books, ugh, of course! I know I shouldn't be greedy and expect much but at least I should get the right level of challenge, no?

CHAPTER 5
ON THE GRIND

"Shami Aunty...I mean, Ms. Shami, I already completed these workbooks back when I attended school. I attended second grade before I stopped school. I am supposed to be in fifth grade so could I please have fifth-grade level workbooks?"

"Nonsense! Your brain must be old and rusty. You must start at the second-grade level and then work your way up. And, besides, I only have Kaveer's stuff to use. So, for fifth-grade level books, you will need to wait until next year when he moves to sixth grade," she explains.

Oh, I understand what she is trying to do. She is

using Kaveer's old junk to teach me. In other words, she isn't willing to buy new books for me. I know she is doing this for free but if she were willing to design the classroom, why would she not want to buy new books for me? I guess the room was more for her than me. What a selfish lady!

"Oh, okay," I mumble.

"Forget about that, let's focus on learning," she opens the book, flips through the pages, and instructs, "I want you to complete the addition and subtraction section."

"But that's easy and like I said, I have already done it before!" I complain.

I know I should be appreciative of her teaching me for free but honestly, asking a fifth-grade student to do addition and subtraction? I know I haven't been to school for three years but that doesn't mean I am still at a second-grade level. That is just not how it works, my friend.

"Then you should be able to do it easily. Start," she orders.

I open my mouth to say something but then stop. There is no use arguing with her. It won't hurt me to do these simple arithmetic problems. But you know when something is so easy that it is actually hard to do? Like it is that uninteresting that you cannot pay attention to it. That is exactly how I feel about this. I decide to suck it up and finish these problems quickly so she can give me something harder.

I quickly speed through the problems. They were easy just as I had said. Honestly, sometimes adults think they know better, but they really don't. They just have that complex in their mind that because they are older, they are wiser.

"I finished. What next?" I ask.

"Wow, you're fast. You must have made some mistakes. Let me check it," she motions for me to hand her the paper.

What is with her not trusting me? She thinks I am dumb, and I can sense it in her tone. I sigh and hand her the paper. She grabs it and starts checking it.

I don't mean to stare at her when I am waiting for my results but there is nothing else to do. She hasn't given me permission to walk around the room, so I have to stay seated. I look straight ahead which is where Shami Aunty is sitting.

As I watch her grade, I notice she is quite distracted. She starts looking at a problem, stares into space around the room, and then goes back to the paper. It is really inefficient. I consider saying something, but I know I must never criticize adults since that is rude. Throughout the process, she also yawns many times and rests her eyes. Due to her sluggish grading, it is a long time before she hands the paper back to me. Normally, grading is supposed to take less time than completing the assignment takes, but it is the opposite here.

"So, how did I do?" I ask.

"Well, all the problems are correct. But it is probably a fluke so keep practicing."

Fluke, my foot! I show her she is wrong and prove my worth, but she still doesn't admit it. What an egotistical woman! No matter how many problems I get correct, I have a feeling she will never admit her assumption was wrong and that I am intelligent.

"Hang on. I need to use the restroom. I will give you more problems when I get back. Until then, stay seated and don't touch *anything*."

She walks up and slowly exits the room. Then, it is just me, alone, in this colorful dream room. There are so many toys and books. I am tempted to get up and take a closer look at them. But I know that if I get caught, it is my second strike of being a disobedient, bad child. The first being the paint incident from when I was younger. I am shocked she still hasn't mentioned it. Adults love talking about stupid things you did as a child to embarrass you. They never seem to forget.

I look up at the bright clock above the whiteboard. I wait five minutes - then ten. Boy, she is taking a long time in the bathroom. Normally, it shouldn't take longer than ten minutes. But I guess everyone's different.

Finally, after twenty long minutes, she comes back. She looks relieved and has a smile on her face. Maybe she will be nicer to me now.

The next few hours go by as slow as honey. Shami Aunty keeps giving me the easiest worksheets. It sucks that we only do Math. If I had it my way, we would do some Math, Science, English, Social Studies, and Hindi alternating through them.

I suggest, "Could we please do different subjects instead of all Math? Perhaps English or Science?"

She asks, "What is the rush? You and I are going to be spending a lot of time together so we can slowly go through all the subjects."

"Well, it is just that I think it is more interesting to cover a bit of one subject and a bit of another like we do in school."

"I don't like doing bits and pieces like that but if you really want to," she hesitates, "we can do Math now and do English and Science in the afternoon."

That deal was fair enough, so I agree. The hope that we would be switching to a different subject pushed me to work harder and faster. Knowing how clever Shami Aunty is, promising a switch of subjects was probably her strategy to motivate me.

Suddenly a load thunderous noise booms through the room. I am worried as to what it is.

Shami Aunty blushes and apologizes, "Sorry, Nikitha, that was my stomach rumbling. I'm hungry. What about you?"

CHAPTER 6
LUNCH TIME

I glance at the clock again. It is exactly 1 pm. This is the time I usually eat at home. Every afternoon, I return to our hut and eat the food Ma left for me. Ma usually takes Kanna to the river to wash clothes and they eat together there. At times, I am jealous that they get to spend that special time together, but I had Ma to myself before Kanna was born. I had Pa too. It makes me sad to think Kanna will never get to know Pa until he gets released which could be many years. Kanna will be a big boy or maybe even a man then.

I realize I am feeling quite hungry. But then my

stomach is in a knot because I know I should return home to eat. How am I going to explain that to Shami Aunty?

"Yes, but I should go back home. Ma would have made something for me. I will quickly run there and back."

"No, no, I can't let you do that. Please eat here with me," she demands.

I knew this would happen. If there is one thing Indians are experts at, it is hospitality. They never let a guest leave without eating or drinking anything and if it is mealtime, they must stay for the meal. There is no way Shami Aunty is going to let *me* go, especially as I am her student. I should have brought the food from home in a tiffin box like school. Ma and I completely forgot about that. Now I am in such a pickle.

"Please let me go. I can't let Ma's food go to waste."

"Who said anything about it being wasted? You can eat it for dinner. It must take a while for you to go back, and you will have to eat alone at home."

"It really isn't that far. I eat alone everyday so no problem. I will be back before you know it."

"Fine but if you go, I will have to eat alone and I hate doing that. Kaveer is at school and his dad is working. Please stay for me," she guilt-trips.

I sigh and reply, "Alright, fine, I'll stay."

I am tired of arguing. I know she could easily find someone else to eat with, but she wants to eat with me so badly. If Ma asks and I know she will, I will simply tell her that Shami Aunty did not allow me to come back home and forced me to eat there. That is more or less the truth.

We walk downstairs together and as I follow her, I truly realize how slow she is. She literally waddles from side to side like a giant penguin. I don't say anything though since that's rude. She shows me to a white marble dining table, and we sit down.

"What would you like to eat, dear?" she asks.

"I'm fine with anything," I reply.

I shouldn't be eating here in the first place so I definitely shouldn't be demanding a specific food.

"Well, we have a world-renowned chef who can cook anything you desire."

"Really?" I ask.

She just puts that out there like it is so casual. A world-renowned chef, wow! I shouldn't be too shocked since Kaveer's family is so rich, but I never knew this or took time to consider it.

"Oh, yes! Chef, please come out here," Shami Aunty calls.

An older man with salt and pepper hair walks out of the kitchen. He is really tall and has a white chef's hat and apron on. He looks intimidating until he smiles.

"Nikitha, this is Chef Arnold. He has cooked all around the world and can make almost anything for you. Chef Arnold, this is Nikitha, the student I am teaching."

He bows and says, "Hello, miss."

"Hello...," I say, shyly.

I am not used to this level of respect like I am actually worth something. Usually, I am the one who must respect others. He is probably forced to bow down and greet all guests though. So, I'm nothing special.

"What is your dream dish, sweetie?" Shami Aunty asks.

I contemplate it for a while. I am not used to dreaming especially when it comes to food. I eat whatever is put in front of me without complaining. Even when Pa was with us, we were still quite poor, so we ate simple dishes like leftover rice, chapati, and curry. Suddenly, I remember a fond memory.

When I was younger, Pa would take me to the supermarket in the city. Back when we still had his salary, we were able to buy things from there instead of the local grocery market Ma goes to now.

One day, he came home early from work, so he took me on his motorcycle to the supermarket. It was my first time going but little did I know it would become my favorite place. Once we reached there, he held my hand, and we walked into the colorful store with bright lights. There were so many aisles, each one dedicated to a specific thing.

"What would you like to buy, Nikku?" he asked me.

"I don't know, Pa...Hey, look at that! What does that mean?" I pointed at a sign that said, "International Cuisine".

He analyzed it and replied, "Nikku, that aisle has food from all around the world not just India. Let's check it out!"

This was highly unusual. As a little girl, I didn't realize how big the world really was and that there were more countries than just India. I grew up eating Indian food and I didn't know other food existed, so I never wished for anything else.

We walked past many cuisines including the Italian pasta and pizzas and Chinese noodles and fried rice. The thing that caught my eye was in the refrigerators. It was a packet with chicken wings covered in crispy breadcrumbs. It looked delicious.

"I want this please!" I exclaimed, pointing to it, and jumping up and down.

We are pure vegetarian so we cannot even eat egg let alone chicken. Pa did not know what to say.

"Uh, Nikku, you do know that we're vegetarian,

right?" he asked.

I put on a face of confusion. Now, I am familiar with vegetarianism but back then I had never heard of it.

"Oh, looks like we never talked to you about it. Today's the day, I guess. Do you at least know what meat is?"

I nodded, "Meat are things like chicken, fish, and beef."

"Yes, meat is any flesh of an animal. We are Hindus, so..."

"Hindus?" I furrowed my eyebrow.

Pa explained, "You know how we go to the temple and Ma does pooja at home? Well, that is how we pray or worship our Hindu gods. We follow the religion, Hinduism, including all its beliefs. One big one is not killing animals which is why we are vegetarian."

"But when we eat meat, we aren't killing animals. They already come dead, right?" I reasoned.

"I know it is hard to understand but eating meat is a sin or a big mistake for us. Do you understand?"

I nodded and as he pulled me away, I looked longingly at the chicken wing package. Then I noticed a bright red cross over a cartoon of meat. I realized that it is vegetarian, after all!

"Pa, look!" I dragged him back to the chicken tenders and pointed to the cartoon.

After he comprehended it, he asked, "Wait, so there isn't chicken in *chicken* tenders? That doesn't make any sense."

He grabbed the package and read the back, the confusion slowly disappearing from his face.

"So, it's vegetarian right?" I confirmed.

"Yes, yes, it is! In fact, every item of this brand is

vegetarian. The cool thing is they all taste as if they are made from meat. But they're not."

"How is that possible, Pa?"

"At first, I didn't understand either, Nikku, but apparently engineers make them."

"Oh, engineers like you?"

"Kind of, but I am a civil engineer. I design infrastructure like buildings and transportation. The people that make meatless meat are genetic engineers. They use soybean plants and extract the DNA to create artificial flavoring. It is truly a fascinating process."

"Okay, well I still don't understand, but if this brand is all vegetarian, could we please get more meals?" I pleaded.

He agreed and we proceeded to look at the other items. After extensive debate, we settled on some shrimp fried rice and mini beef hotdogs along with the chicken tenders. It was great - we would know the taste of meat without breaking Hindu laws. The only drawback was that it was expensive. In fact, it was so expensive that we couldn't afford anything else. Ma sent us to buy lentils, rice, vegetables, and milk but we didn't buy any of those items. We decided to risk it and returned home with these three fancy meatless packages. We knew we would be in big trouble with Ma. We shuddered with fear as we stepped into the kitchen.

"Oh, good, you're back! I was planning on making lentils and rice with potato curry. Hope you bought all the groceries," she looked at the bag with curiosity, "One bag fit all the items? Must be magical then!"

Pa set the bag on the counter and Ma emptied it, realizing our mistake. She glared furiously at the items and back at us.

"What is this?" she questioned, in her serious

voice.

We looked down, embarrassed to tell her the truth.

"Answer me! I send you to the store to buy our grocery essentials and you return with three frozen meat packages! What were you thinking?!"

"Shh, shh, Kamla, don't scream, the neighbors can hear you," Pa tried to quiet her.

"Let them hear. It is your fault for doing this. So stupid! Did you leave your brains at home or something?"

"Okay, enough. Let me explain what happened. We were going to buy our groceries and passed through the frozen aisle where we saw these *vegetarian* packages."

Ma is baffled, "Vegetarian? What do you take me for - a fool? Obviously, this is chicken, shrimp, and ew, beef. As Hindus, we cannot eat this, and you know it."

"That's what we thought, too, but they are a fancy type of vegetarian meat. They taste like meat but are safe for Hindus. Some new discovery," Pa explained.

"Really? Well, then I guess it is okay but that sounds expensive. How much was each one?"

"Hundred rupees," he mumbled.

"Wait, what?" Ma asked in disbelief.

"Ma, he said each package cost one hundred rupees each," I replied, enunciating each word, and not understanding the situation.

Ma went pale and held the counter to keep her balance. She looked as if she had seen a ghost.

"Kamla, please calm down."

"Krishna, how can I calm down if you spend three hundred rupees - almost our entire grocery quota for this week - on this rubbish!"

Angrily, I defend Pa, "It's not rubbish, Ma. They look delicious."

"Nikku, quiet, let me handle this. Kamla, I should have thought this through, I know, but we can figure something out," Pa assured.

"Like what? Starving for a whole week?"

"No, no, I will go to the market tomorrow and buy the groceries we need. They have cheaper prices there. In the meantime, we can eat this special food. What do you want tonight, Nikku?"

"Can we have chicken tenders please?" I ask.

Chicken tenders were my favorite and after that meal, I have been dreaming about my next chance to eat them to this day. After dinner that night, there was one more huge problem, though. We didn't have a fridge let alone a freezer to cool the packages. This just caused more conflict between my parents.

Eventually, Pa got the idea to put them into a box and bury them underground. The ground temperature is far colder, so he promised they would be fine. He is such a clever engineer!

After that incident, our life just became so hard that I could never eat what I wanted - those chicken tenders. I have finally gotten an excellent opportunity. But would asking for these soy-based chicken tenders be too much? I decide to give it a try.

CHAPTER 7
A PLEASED CHEF

"Could I please have chicken tenders without meat?" I ask.

Shami Aunty laughs and explains, "Nikitha, chicken tenders have to be made from chicken, which is meat, but that was a funny joke!"

My cheeks turn red in embarrassment. I wasn't joking!

"I think I understand what you mean, madam. Are you asking for soy-based meatless chicken tenders?" Chef Arnold asks.

"Yes Chef, is that possible?" I ask, skeptically.

"Of course, but all you have to do for that is heat up a frozen package. You could make that at home itself," he reasons.

I wish I could make it at home. It is just way out of our economic zone right now. I don't know what to say so I look at Shami Aunty, hoping she will understand.

"Chef, please prepare whatever she wants."

He bows and walks back into the kitchen.

"I can't help but ask, dear, why as a vegetarian did you want chicken tenders? Even though they are meatless."

"Ms. Shami, people always tend to want what they can't have in life. Like how I can't taste chicken since I'm vegetarian, so I want to try this alternative method to taste it."

"I see. Those are some wise words of wisdom!"

A few moments later, Chef Arnold enters with two plates in his hands. He sets one in front of each of us. I have gotten the crispiest, delectable chicken tenders ever! My mouth waters just looking at them. They look even better than they did all those years ago. I don't know how that is since both were from a frozen package. But possibly, they are a higher quality brand since the store they get their groceries from is more expensive.

I glance over at Shami Aunty, and she is already stuffing her face full of hakka noodles and crunching on the veggies loudly. I notice Chef Arnold looking at me with concern. Oh no, he thinks I am not eating his food because I don't like it. I immediately dive in and finish the entire plate within minutes.

"Wow, you're a fast eater. I assume you liked it," Shami Aunty chuckles.

"Liked it? I absolutely loved it! Chef Arnold is the greatest chef ever!" I exclaim.

Then, I get up to hug him. He looks awestruck to receive this praise and attention.

"Ha, thank you, but this is basic. I could make you something far more sophisticated from France. That is where I am from. How about tarte tatin or quiche?"

"Nikitha will be coming for class daily so looks like you can wow her with more of your cooking, Chef," Shami Aunty tells him.

"Uh, Ms. Shami, I think from now on I will bring the lunch Ma makes for me. That is better for all of us and Ma would prefer that as well. Sorry," I apologize.

"Alright, that's fair. I am also sorry for forcing you to eat here today. Hope it didn't make you feel too uncomfortable."

"No, no, not at all. It was fun. A pleasant change from my daily routine...also, I am wondering, how did Chef know you wanted hakka noodles?"

"Because it is what madam eats daily, Nikitha!" Chef Arnold exclaims and we all burst out laughing.

I think to myself, "Noodles everyday can't possibly be healthy."

After we finish eating and wash our hands, we return back upstairs to continue learning.

"In the morning, you showed me you have understood Math quite well, so excellent job on that. Now as I promised, we can switch subjects. You pick!"

"Really?" I ask, astonished.

So far, Shami Aunty has been an extreme control freak. I never expected her to give me the freedom to choose.

"Yes, of course. It is your learning. I may have

been controlling this morning and I'm sorry, but I needed to get to know you. I trust you now."

"Oh, wow, thanks. Could we do Science please?" I request.

"Sure, good choice," she hands me a workbook, "Here you go."

I see it is also a second-grade book, but I don't complain. I love all types of science, especially biology since it is about living things. It seems so exciting to discover new things about how the world works. This is why I loved exploring the village so much. Every day I could observe the beauties of the world, powered by science.

"Before you start, I just wanted to clarify that Science is not as straightforward as Math and you must recall information. There are explanations in the workbook, but if you still don't understand, feel free to ask me."

I nod and start reading about food webs. Before I know it, I am in the sixth chapter about types of rocks. This workbook is good because it has vocabulary definitions and connects to the real world. The appearance with the colors and pictures enhances the reading experience too.

"Okay, I'm going to take a small nap. That lunch was too good," Shami Aunty yawns and nods off right at her desk.

I expected she would at least go sleep in her bed as this is her house. I dread every minute of her sleeping because she snores - loudly! It literally sounds like a bulldozer in the room. It is *so* bad I can't focus. I quietly go outside so I can concentrate on my work.

When I sit in the open area outside, there is an eerie feeling of being alone. Probably because we are in a giant mansion. I wish more people were here though. It would be livelier.

I dismiss those creepy feelings and work my way
through the rest of the workbook until I am done. After,
I check my work with the answer key in the back. It is
mostly correct except for some minor errors because I
didn't understand the wording of the question. Maybe
we should review English first because I have gotten
weak in it, haha!

Just then, Shami Aunty comes out of the room
and sees me, "Nikitha! What are you doing here?"

"I finished the workbook and corrected it."

"That's good, but why did you come out here?
The room is your classroom from now on. You should
do your work there."

"Sorry, Ms. Shami. I just wanted a change of
space. I was going to ask you, but I didn't want to
disturb your sleep."

That was a lie, but I can't tell her that it was
because of her annoyingly loud snoring. I should have

been more careful to check when she woke up though. I guess I was too distracted by science.

"Oh, well from now on please stay in the classroom. It is a lot easier for me to manage you there. Anyway, could I see your workbook?"

"I checked it with the answer key. I understood all my mistakes," I reason.

"I still want to see it. Hand it over, please."

"Why don't you trust me?!" I accidentally yell at her.

CHAPTER 8
MIXTURE MANIA

She looks shocked. In Hinduism, we are supposed to worship our parents and teachers even before God. I am such a bad person for yelling at Ms. Shami. After all, she is my teacher.

"My bad, I didn't mean to yell but to be honest, I don't like when you always doubt me."

"Oh, I'm really sorry. I guess I never realized how it seemed like I was doubting you. It is not your fault. I treat you like how I treat everyone. I have taught Kaveer before. Ask him if I doubt him or not. It may be a little extra for you since I'm not used to teaching you, but I'll surely try to change," she promises.

Wow. She is actually a good person. All I needed to do is just talk to her freely about what is bothering me.

Shami Aunty tells me, "And I don't need to see it that badly. I trust you if you think you understand all of it."

I thank her. I am glad we talked about this. If not, both of us would have suffered for much longer.

"I think it is time for a break, Nikitha," she starts.

"Oh, but I'm not tired," I reply, ignorant.

"Haha, *I* am though. Sorry but I am used to napping most of the day. Let's go downstairs and eat some snacks while watching television."

I follow her back downstairs, but I am not happy about it. I wanted to get through English before doing anything else. She has not even taught me a single lesson and only made me do workbook pages for a few hours. Besides, it feels like we just ate lunch, and she is snacking already.

"Come, follow me into the pantry," she leads me.

I enter their pantry, and it is huge - bigger than my whole hut! It resembles the supermarket, shelves full of foreign goodies and treats.

"What would you like to snack on, dear?" she asks.

I take a second to absorb all the options. It is still way too much for me!

"Sorry, I have never seen these many snacks in one room before. It's a lot to take in."

"Oh, I understand. Well, I can start you off today with some of Kaveer's favorites. Since you both are the same age, maybe your food palates are the same too," she suggests.

That is some chopped logic. Kaveer's taste is weird like all boys my age. But I wait to see what she selects for me.

She grabs a cute mini shopping basket like the

ones at the store and fills it up with a bunch of snacks.
She puts in chocolate cookies, cheese crackers, dried
mangoes, plantain chips and more. Everything looks
delicious! Once again, I feel guilty for not bringing my
own food and leeching on Shami Aunty's food. I notice
she keeps filling the basket.

"No, please, that's enough," I stop her, trying to
grab the basket.

"Nonsense. That can't possibly last you. Is that
really all you eat?" she asks.

It is unfortunate but the portion sizes we have
been eating have drastically decreased after Pa left. We
simply couldn't afford proper nourishment and had to
eat the bare minimum to survive. We got used to eating
less so our appetites significantly reduced.

I nod and say, "I will see which ones I like."

She agrees and looks around for her mixture.
Mixture is an Indian delicacy that is a mix of flattened
rice, nuts, spices, curry leaves, and corn flakes. It is the

go-to snack in every Indian household.

"Oh, no! Looks like we have run out of mixture. The grocery servant must have missed it during the check this morning...Oh, wait, I finished it after the check. Oops."

This family really values their snacks so much that they have a servant whose job is to take an inventory of all the snacks and ensure they are filled every day. That is ridiculous.

Shami Aunty looks at me and starts hyperventilating and freaking out. Yikes.

"Calm down, Ms. Shami. It is not a big deal. Just mixture. You can eat something else."

"No! Nikitha, you don't understand. Mixture is literally all I eat except my three meals. I cannot settle for any other snack. What do we do?"

"We could go buy some more at the store," I suggest.

"Oh, right. Why didn't I think of that? I wish I

could go to the store, but I can't leave you home alone and all the servants have left for their lunch break...Sweetie, how about you go to the shop and get a packet of mixture for me?" she asks.

This doesn't make any sense. If she doesn't want to leave me home alone, how is she okay with letting me go to the store by myself? That is far more dangerous!

"Please do me this solid, Nikitha."

This is so strange. I never saw myself buying mixture for my teacher who is supposed to be teaching me. She is addicted to it, and I am concerned. Her craze is scaring me. If I refuse, I wonder what she will do to me. I guess it will be nice to get some fresh air and see the outside world. Inside Kaveer's house, there is a weird feeling of being disconnected.

"Okay, sure," I agree.

"That's a good sport!" she exclaims.

We walk to the front of the house, and she grabs her purse. From there, she hands me a hundred rupees!

I am in shock just holding that much money. It must be peanuts for rich folks like Ms. Shami. Ma toils so hard for even a portion of it.

"Why so much money? A mixture packet only costs twenty rupees."

"I know that but please buy five packets, so we don't run out easily. I hate the feeling of not having a mixture. I need it!"

Now, she is starting to sound like a true addict. I take the money and leave. On my way out, it seems peculiarly strange. There is not even a single person outside. Normally, in our part of the village there are always people bustling through the streets. I guess in these sophisticated neighborhoods, the aunties and uncles like to stay inside and enjoy the comfort of their homes like Ms. Shami. If my house were a palace like theirs, maybe I would be inside all the time, too.

I put on my sandals and look around. Where is the watchman? I have only seen him once, yet the entrance seems empty without him. I look to the left and see a sign. It says, "WATCHMAN ON BREAK". Oh, I see!

The gate is slightly open, so I crawl out and walk. Everyone in this town area is unfamiliar, so I feel like an impostor, out of place. Near home, I know everyone from the vegetable vendor to the cycle rickshaw uncle. I always wave at my "friends" and smile. I am starting to realize that sometimes, being near your loved ones outweighs being rich. It is a kind of joy you can find nowhere else.

CHAPTER 9
COWS

I keep going and the signs of a suburban neighborhood, the houses, shops, and cars, slowly start to fade away. Soon, all I see around me is rough, grainy grass that is the color of sand. It is so brown that grass is too much of a compliment for it; it should be called hay. It looks like no farmer owns this land because otherwise it would not have been so unkempt and dry.

The villagers I know worship the land and soil, spending so much energy caring for it and keeping it green. In return, they reap the gifts of the land - whether it is fresh produce or grains - and make money to run their families and are able to feed the population.

Along with the lack of civilization, I also notice that there aren't any people around here. I had been walking on a straight dirt path which started at the end of the town. The two plots of land on either side of me are polar opposites. On the right, I see miles and miles of barren land; it is such a pitiable sight. On the left, the grass is an assortment of greens and browns and grown unevenly. I start feeling lonely and oddly vulnerable being in the center of this area.

As I look down, I see a bright pink arrow drawn leading ahead. Who would draw this and what is it leading to? Several feet ahead, there is another one. I debate whether I should follow them. It could be dangerous, and I hear Ma's voice in my mind warning me not to do it since it is risky. Quiet, Ma, life is an adventure, when else am I going to get the chance to come this far away from home?

After I come across six of those pink arrows, what

I find came as a bolt from the blue. I see a group of around forty cows inside a fenced wooden pen, covered by a tarp shelter. The cows are in all colors: brown, white, black, and mixed. From a distance, I froze as my jaw dropped upon looking at them, but I decide to go closer to get a better look.

As I approach them, I realize something is wrong. The cows look very unwell, probably a combination of exhaustion and sickness. A lot of them are resting on the ground or staring off into space. I look at many of them and notice they don't have the glimmer in their eyes that most cows do. Worst of all, the entire pen is so filthy and disgusting!

In a large box at the front of the pen, there appears to be remnants of hay and dirty water. None of the cows even seem to be coming near the box. Most likely, they haven't eaten or drank in days. I mean, who can blame them when their options are either consuming bacteria or nothing at all?

On the ground, there is cow dung everywhere! I feel like vomiting so I cannot imagine how the cows must be feeling, having to live here all the time. Even though they are animals, they still deserve a level of cleanliness and hygiene. There is an awful, unpleasant odor in the air, but I can't tell if it is from the food and water box or the cow dung.

I pet some of the cows closer to me and can literally feel their bones. They are malnourished - this is an outrage! I walk around the pen to the back corner and see a sight that would make anyone's heart ache.

This brown calf, hardly a month old, is lying on the ground, struggling to breathe. Her mother is sitting next to her, looking so concerned. She is making cow noises that sound like cries. Both seem to be in so much pain. I stroke the calf on the head a few times, trying to comfort her, but it is hard for me to reach through the fence.

I can tell she will not last much longer. I feel bad

that her fate led her to having to live in such a horrible situation. I wish I could take her to a veterinarian so she can receive medical care and survive. It feels horrible just standing here as a spectator on the outside, unable to do anything to help.

I take a few steps back to assess the whole situation. This pen is not even close to enough square footage for so many living beings. The cows barely have enough room to walk a few steps or lie on the ground. In fact, there actually would not be enough space for all of them to lie down and sleep simultaneously.

The poor cows are trapped here. It is animal cruelty and must be reported to the government. Unfortunately, animal rights are often neglected, so the case will not be prioritized or focused on. If only I get my hands on whoever owns these cows, then I will not let them go free.

Just as I think that thought, a truck starts driving towards the pen. Before I am seen, I quickly run further into the field and crouch into the grass to hide myself. The truck pulls up and two men get out of it. One of them is tall and muscular while the other one is slightly shorter with a big beard. Simply by looking at them, I can tell they are dangerous guys with whom I should not mess.

My heart races from my anxiety that they will spot me, and I might get in big trouble. I hope for the best and decide to observe what they are doing.

The tall guy asks the short guy, "What do you think, Abdul master? How are the cows looking?"

Abdul replies, "They look rather skinny and there is not a lot of flesh on them. I want to sell juicy steaks not scraps. Why are they so lean?"

"I don't know, master. I am giving them plenty of food, but they won't eat. They are very stubborn."

Oh, really? What a liar. He claims to be feeding the cows, but this cheap hay is not enough for them. It is not fit for a living thing to consume. They must be so sick of this nasty plant that they don't eat - they are not the ones to blame. They should be fed fresh grasses and fruits along with good-quality hay.

Back in the village, the farmers worship their cows and feed them the best food. In fact, in the Hindu religion, cows are sacred, and each part of the cow is a god. Instead of this mistreatment, these guys should be cherishing their cows. They are the lucky ones to be able to reap the benefits of these divine animals.

"Nonsense! I know you are wasting the money I am giving for cow food on your own stuff, let me see this so-called food," Abdul opens the pen gate and walks toward the food box, "Come here, eat this!"

The cow he is talking to does not even move an inch, being so terrified. I have heard that larger, more developed animals like cows can feel human emotions just like us. One doesn't need half a brain to understand that Abdul has bad intentions. Poor animal probably does not realize that by not obeying his master, he will end up in bigger trouble.

"Eat this, you animal, can't you hear me?!" he screams.

He is hostile and shoves the hay in the cow's face, yelling at the cow to eat. What is the poor thing going to understand? All the cows shudder in fear. This is no owner; he is a true monster.

Right then, I see the side above me that says, "ABDUL'S BEEF FARM". I am shocked. All these cows are going to be slaughtered and eaten as beef? This is horrible! I must do something to save them.

I look back to Abdul and the cows. After he has forced some of them into eating the hay, he is satisfied.

"You lot better be eating the food we feed you every day or you will be killed...well, actually all of you are going to be butchered one day anyway, haha!" he cackles like a maniac.

My heart sinks after hearing those mean words. I bet the only reason this Abdul guy has this farm is to torture the animals. He seems like the kind of person to take pleasure in such horrible deeds.

"Hey, you, make sure you do this every day. I am not paying you to be the cow caretaker for no reason. You have to work worthy of your pay, got it? If not you, I can easily find another worker, understand?" Abdul yells at the tall guy.

He has his head hung down, "Yes, sir. I understand. I will make sure they are always eating their meals. You just wait, the next time you pay a visit, they will have fattened up nicely."

"They better have! Eid is coming up in a few weeks, so we will need a lot of meat soon. It is your responsibility for us to be able to fill those orders. Hmmph," Abdul grunts and walks back to the car.

His servant frowns at the cows, "Look at what you idiots have done. Now, Abdul sir is angry at me because *you* didn't eat."

He kicks the gate shut and stomps back to the car.

As they leave, I watch their car slowly drive off into the distance. I get out from my hiding spot and look at the cows. They are still in shock from those mean men. At least, I am glad they left instead of staying longer. I look back at the sick calf who stole my heart. She still looks the same. I decide to quietly open the gate and sit next to her.

Walking into the pen, I am kind of scared. Even though these cows are not in decent shape, each one of them weighs at least a thousand pounds. My puny body could never withstand their weight. I trust that they have good intentions, but if something goes wrong, it could lead to serious problems.

This calf is more important than my fears, so I carefully walk over to her, making it clear that I am not a threat. Luckily, the cows all pay no attention to me and simply mind their own business. I slowly sit down beside the calf and allow her to rest her head on my legs. Her mother looks at me in suspicion for a few moments but then lets me stay. I stroke the calf's head.

She looks up and smiles at me. I can sense my love, and

attention is making her feel better. Being here makes

me   feel   content,   too.

CHAPTER 10
THE REAL AUNTY

A while later, I remember that the whole reason Shami Aunty sent me is to get mixture and I have to return in a reasonable amount of time, or she will start to worry. I pet the calf whom I named Soniya one more time and get up. Her fur is golden just like the real *sona* (gold) so I chose the name Soniya. I realize I should not have named her because when you name something, you will become more attached, but I didn't know what to call her.

I make my way out of the pen and as I am about to close the gate, a part of me doesn't want to trap these animals again. I want to open the gate and let them free.

They would finally get a taste of freedom!

Although, once reality kicks in, I decide not to since myself and my family would get in big trouble. Once Abdul found out, he would severely punish us.

"Guys, I promise I will free you so you can all live happy lives but please be patient. I have to leave for today, but I will be back. I promise," I tell them.

It takes all my willpower to leave the cows, but I have no choice. I return back on the same dirt path. When I reach the start of the town, I continue to walk, with the money in my pocket, looking around for a tea shop. I am used to seeing tea shops lining every street and road with people sitting in front of them, chatting their days away.

Tea shops are ingrained in our culture and are very versatile. Villagers use them for way more than just buying chai but socialize in the community and buy snacks there. For me, it is the only place to find my favorite candy, sweet tamarind chews. I cannot get enough of their tangy and sour flavor! It just keeps me wanting more. I guess I love tamarind candy as much as Shami Aunty loves mixture - which is why I need to find it soon.

My default place to buy mixture would have been a tea shop, but oddly enough, there are barely any around these parts. Even the shops that are there are closed due to lunch break. Between 2-4 pm, everything is closed so people can go home, eat their lunches, and take a nice nap. I should have considered this or checked with Shami Aunty before leaving her house. Now, she would be waiting with the hope that I will return with mixture; if I don't, she'll be crushed. I decide to ask around to the few folks who are roaming around at that time. I see a middle-aged woman walking in the street, wearing an orange sari and a big smile.

"Excuse me, Aunty, do you know where I can find mixture?" I ask.

She keeps on walking and smiling, not even

looking at me. Can she not see or hear me? I consider that she may be ignoring me, but there is no reason to as we have never met before. No one can pretend that they cannot hear this well. I decide to not give up on her and follow her.

"Aunty, Aunty! Hello!" I yelled.

There is no response again. Eventually, after chasing her a bit farther I tap her shoulder, and she looks behind at me. She removes two plastic objects from her ears, one from each side.

"Hi, Aunty. I have been calling your name and following you for a while now."

"Hello, dear. Sorry, I was wearing my earbuds so I could not hear you," she explains.

"Earbuds, what are those?" I ask, puzzled.

"Oh, they are these devices," she holds up the plastic objects, "I connect them to my phone and play whatever music I want. I can use them to listen on the go. The only downside is I can't hear outside noises like you calling when I am wearing them."

"Ah, I see, they seem super cool! Where did you get it, Aunty? Are they distributing it in the village quota?"

"No, no, of course not, dear. They would never give out such expensive items in the quota. My brother-in-law brought it from America during his last visit here."

"Oh, I see. Your brother-in-law lives in America? That is so cool. What is it like there?" I ask, with curiosity.

By this point, I have learned about the many countries of the world and always wanted to live in America. It seemed like the world's best place filled with celebrities and luxuries. I wish I got the chance to move there or at least experience life there for a few days.

"I have never been there myself, but my brother tells me that it is not that different from India."

"Really? That's surprising since all I have heard

is that it is like a different world there with palaces lining all the streets and rich people everywhere. Where does your brother-in-law live?"

"He lives in Boston, Massachusetts. The winters are freezing there, and it snows a few feet...I know all the villagers here talk about the wonders of America and I agree, it is a wonderful place to live, but it isn't the polar opposite of India. Sure, the weather is way colder as it is higher north and everything is of higher quality, but there are poor people there, too."

Now, that shocks me. "I always thought everyone there was rich and well-off. I mean how else would they be able to move there?"

"Well, you are referring to immigrants from other countries like India but there are residents that are from the United States itself. Often times, they can suffer in poverty. I don't blame you for thinking this way since that is the picture media and magazines has built in our minds. In fact, I used to be envious of my brother-in-law for living in America while I was stuck here too, but after I heard stories of what it is like there, I am happy to live in the comfort of our village. You should be, too. Anyway, what is your name and why were you calling me?"

"My name is Nikitha. I am looking for mixture for my teacher. I don't live around here, so I was not sure where to look. Could you please help me?"

"Of course, my child. I am Raji and I am a native of this area. You can call me Raji Aunty. For mixture, there aren't very many tea shops here, but you are in luck! My neighbor makes homemade mixture. It is cheap and tastes amazing. I can take you to her and you can buy the mixture if you want to...I wanted to ask, where are you from?"

"Palakkad," I reply.

"Oh, really, that is where I grew up! I only moved here after marriage...Wait, then I probably know your parents. What are their names?" she asks.

"My mom's name is Kamla and..."

She interrupts me, "Oh, my goodness. Are you Kamla's daughter?"

I nod and she bends down, holding my hands and looking into my eyes.

"My word! You look just like her - a carbon copy," she is awestruck.

I have been told many times before that I look like my mom. Whenever I look into the mirror, I realize it is kind of true. I have her eyes, nose, and lips. We even have the same beauty spot on our chins. But I wonder why Raji Aunty is so surprised to see me and still holding my hands.

She notices I am feeling uncomfortable by her gesture and lets me go, "Sorry, I am just surprised since your mother, and I were so close back in the day. You could call us best friends. I haven't seen her in years, though," she sighs.

I can't believe what I am hearing! This is the first

time I have met one of Ma's childhood friends. Whenever I asked her about her school days and friends, she would dismiss the conversation. I wonder what occurred that was so bad she does not want to talk about it. I guess meeting Raji Aunty is good to at least find out the answer to that question if nothing else.

"Really, is that true, Aunty? That's shocking since Ma never mentions her childhood. How did you guys meet?" I ask.

"That is so typical of Kamla. She has not changed one bit. Even when I knew her, she was super reserved and serious - never liked to reflect on the past and feel nostalgic. I don't exactly remember when we first met but I think it was in preschool. Actually, she is my second cousin, so we connected as relatives, as well. We really have known each other forever."

Second cousin, wow! That makes Raji Aunty my real aunt. All this time I have been calling older women 'Aunty' to show respect, but in this case it is true. I inquire some more and find out that my grandma, Ma's mother, and Raji Aunty's mother are sisters, making them second cousins. So, Raji Aunty's children would be my third cousins. Finally, I have the chance to have a cousin!

With a heart filled of hope, I ask, "Aunty, do you have children? I have always wanted cousins."

She shook her head in dismay, "No kids, dear. My husband passed away years back and I have been living alone."

Immediately, I am hit by a wave of sadness and pity for this woman. By seeing Ma suffer firsthand, I know how hard it can be to live alone; at least she had Kanna and myself, so she was not entirely by herself. It is a completely different case for Raji Aunty. I want to say something consoling but decide against it to avoid making the conversation awkward. What am I supposed to say to this poor woman?

I decide to divert the conversation, "Anyway,

what has stopped my mom and you from meeting all these years?"

At that point, we are standing in front of a small, red brick house. It certainly isn't as lavish as Shami Aunty's palace but far better than our hut. I assume it is Raji Aunty's house as I was not focusing, simply following her lead, and she brought us here.

"Ah, our conversation has taken us home. Come inside and I'll get some tea on the stove. We can chat and I'll answer your question."

I hesitate for a brief moment because I don't want to impose myself on Raji Aunty, but I am too interested in finding out about Ma's past. Besides, it is her friend so she shouldn't get angry at me if I go to her friend's house.

I enter the red wooden door and see the assortment of items on the red coffee table surrounded by red recliner sofas. They vary from photo frames, papers, pens, and other intriguing red objects.

"Wow, you sure do love red!" I exclaim.

"Haha, that's what it looks like, right? But I am not the red lover, it was my husband. All these red items remind me of him, so I still keep them. He was crazy for red and anytime he would see an item that is red, he would bring it home. He has collected everything as you can see," she points at the table.

"That's really fun, why do you think he liked red so much?" I ask.

"I don't know. It was his favorite color, so he started collecting a few objects and it became a habit. In his words exactly, he would say red objects together seemed so beautiful and powerful."

"Yeah, I see what he means," I pause and decide to ask the question, "Aunty, do you ever miss him?"

"What?" she asks, bewildered.

"I mean, do you ever miss Uncle?"

CHAPTER 11
HISTORY LESSON

She stares at one of his photos she just finished dusting and replies, "I won't deny it, I really did miss him. You can ask anyone. I cried harder than I ever have in my entire life when he passed away because I loved him to pieces! It was so unfair, Nikitha, in just a single accident, our whole life shattered. You know what happened that night? Both of us were walking on the road and suddenly a truck came charging towards us.

He leapt in front of me and shoved me aside to protect

me. Though, he was the one who needed protection. He

got severely injured and passed away. I was saved that

night by that hero who loved me so much, he was

willing to sacrifice his life for me," she chokes up and I

hug her.

She continues, "Uncle was a great man, dear. But

that was five years ago and over time, I have learned

that there is no use weeping and wasting away the days.

I need to be strong and fight because that is what he

would have wanted. And he is not completely gone

because he still lives on in here," she points to her heart.

I hug her again and tell her, "It is going to be

okay. Sorry for reminding you about him and making

you cry, Aunty."

"Nonsense! You didn't make me cry. It feels good

thinking about him and reminiscing over our memories

and as I said, his spirit still lives on. I'm not you're your mom and I actually enjoy nostalgia...You know, what the worst thought is when you lose someone? The worry that you might forget them forever."

"I understand what you mean. That is how I feel about my dad. I wish my mom were as brave as you and pushed through with the mindset you have."

"Your mom? What do you mean?" she asks, confused.

Oh, wait, is it possible for me to meet someone who doesn't know about what happened to Pa? All the neighbors and villagers in our area are aware of the incident. Maybe the word has not traveled this far.

"Aunty, did you not hear from Ma or anyone about the incident?" I ask.

"No, I don't know what you are talking about. Like I said, your mother and I stopped talking ages ago so I have been disconnected from her."

"How about you explain the reason for that, and I can tell you about this? I think it'll make more sense if I know what you already know if that makes sense."

"Okay, well, brace yourself. This is quite a long and emotional story especially with you being her daughter."

She starts the story. Ten years ago, Ma and Raji Aunty were very close. Both of their families lived on the same street, so they were neighbors and were able to meet frequently. They were both not sent to school due to lack of funds in the home and so they would spend their time helping out at the family farm. Although they were distant relatives, there were no feuds or issues among them, so the families were close and even owned a joint farm. Farming was a gamble as it really depended on the crops and the season. They did not have great luck, so they were not able to escape their poverty.

One day, Ma and Raji Aunty went to the river to fill out their buckets with freshwater. They were not able to afford the water from the trucks, so they had to make do with the river water.

Normally, no one else would be in those parts but surprisingly that time, they ran into a group of boys. The boys were playing cricket by the side of the river. One boy threw the ball, and another was trying to hit it with the bat. Unfortunately, that boy missed, and the ball came straight towards Ma. She was holding a big bucket which she had just finished filling. As anyone can guess, the ball hit her, and she dropped the bucket causing all the water to pour out.

The boy who bowled the ball came running towards Ma and sincerely apologized. He acted like a gentleman and went to fill up the bucket himself in the river. He made his friends wait because helping my mom was more important.

"I think you already guessed but yeah, that man was your father."

I am awestruck but not too surprised, as it takes someone like Pa to be so friendly and helpful, so I nod in agreement.

"When your dad brought back the bucket and handed it to your mom, she told him he didn't need to, but he said that it was no problem at all. Then, they stared at each other, and I felt the sparks flying! It was love at first sight. After that, your mom was a different person. She couldn't stop smiling and constantly talked to me about him. She fell head over heels for your dad," Raji Aunty chuckles.

I laugh as well. That is the sweetest love story. Raji Aunty continues with what happens next. I am all ears.

She explains how Ma's and Pa's families both had different ideas about marriage. Ma's parents specifically wanted her to marry someone within the village. As Pa was from another side of the state, it was a hard no. On the other hand, Pa's parents wanted him to continue with higher studies before getting settled in life. Their priorities were not aligning so it could never work out.

"Why were my grandparents so picky? Could they not have adjusted for my parents?"

"Yeah, but they each had their own agendas in mind. It also was not good for their status quo if the marriage happened. Plus, your mom's parents did not like your dad very much."

"Seriously, why? When they met my dad, they would have sensed he is a good man, right?" I ask.

"Yeah, I thought they would, too. For a few months after that day by the river, your parents would meet each other in secrecy. I was the only one who knew, and I could spot true love. Your father was a gem of a man, and I knew Kamla was lucky to have him. Eventually, your father had to leave to go back to his hometown. Your parents couldn't bear to say goodbye to each other because they knew that by the next time they met, they both would have got married to someone else. This is why Kamla, and I proposed the idea of your dad to your grandparents the day before he had to leave."

"Then what happened? This story is super hooking like a TV serial. I can't wait to find out what happened next!"

"Ha, yes, but it was all real. When your father came to your mother's house to meet your grandparents, he was extremely polite and carefully asked the question about their marriage. Right then, your mom's parents revealed to her that they already fixed a wedding with another guy and that your dad should not be following your mom around anymore."

I gasp in shock, "No! How could they?!"

"Yeah, I get how you feel. Myself and all the girls felt the exact same way. The way things were going, we were all hoping for their wedding. Once your grandparents said that your mom just burst out right then and there in front of them. She was partly ashamed that your dad had to hear this and angry about the whole situation. I remember that moment when I saw a whole different side of Kamla. Love fueled her with a fiery passion. She yelled at her parents, telling them that she will marry Krishna because she loves him."

"Wow, I can imagine how stunning that would have been to witness," I state.

"Why, yes, but you don't understand. Your mom was a girl who literally never spoke back to her parents. She obeyed them word for word. Defying them in such a manner was never expected of her. In fact, it would be frowned upon by most adults like her parents, but I was proud that she finally decided to live her life for herself."

"For sure, yes! I guess that explains why my grandparents stopped talking to her."

"Yes, but it was way more extreme than that. After she said no to them, they told her that if she did not listen to them, she didn't need to live in their house anymore and be a part of the family. Poor Kamla, her parents practically threatened to disown her. She was faced with a tough decision: Krishna or her parents. She chose Krishna and walked out of her house, holding his hand. The next day, they eloped and left for your father's town, and I haven't seen her since."

"Even if her relationship with my grandparents was ruined, why did you stop talking to her, Aunty?" I ask.

"Nikitha, your grandpa was furious at your mom and told everyone in the family to stop all communication with her. He thought it was a disgrace that she would run away with your dad. He even told my parents to make sure I did not talk to her. It was not all him, though, since the hatred was mutual – your mom never came back to apologize either. To avoid causing any problems, I did not reach out to her. But that doesn't mean that I have forgotten her, not at all. Often, I think about her and whether she is doing okay. I just trust that she would be living a good life because I have faith in your father and his ability to care for her...Now, what were you saying about your dad, is he doing well?" she asks.

CHAPTER 12
THE WALK

After she has said so much, how do I break it to her that Pa is in jail and our family is suffering? She will feel devastated for Ma. But I know I can't lie to her either because she will be living with the false hope that will be crushed the day, she finds out the truth. Just like it happened to me.

I narrate the entire situation end to end with

parts of what happened before and after for context. It sure is odd for me to do this because I have never had to tell the story to someone. People around me already found out so I never had the need to.

I finish by explaining how it has been so difficult to bail Pa out that Ma has temporarily given up on that. I tell her that I wish we could save him somehow.

She takes a couple minutes to process everything and takes a deep breath. I thought she would be used to shocking news, but I guess that isn't possible. Finding out your best friend's life was ruined must hurt.

"Aunty, are you okay? I understand this is a lot to take in and although it is all true, we are trying to get back on our feet. Ma has improved quite a bit from when Pa was first arrested," I try to console her but fail.

"Nikitha, oh my gosh, I don't know what to say. I am imagining what happened and I just want to cry," she tears up, "Kamla must have been so disappointed when your father was arrested. I know how much she loved him. They both loved each other. And I can only imagine how hard it must have been for you, as a child, to see all of this, dear. You guys should have reached out to me earlier. I would have tried my best to help."

"Aunty, if the family were closer with us, it would have been much easier then. We would have had a support system. Only after talking to you do I understand the real reason why both sides of my family have rejected us. You know, Ma reached out to family members with the hope that they would lend money, but it was of no use. Most of them did not answer and those that did, badly scolded her. Even knowing the state we were in, they ignored us," I cry.

"Don't cry," Raji Aunty hugs me, "It's okay. I am here now. I am not sure if your mom came to see me, but I definitely would not have ignored her. She probably just reached out to people who had money to loan unlike me," she says, sadly.

"What do you mean?" I ask, confused, "I thought

you were well-off judging by your appearance and house. Is that...not so?"

"That's what everyone thinks, and it is partially true. We were financially stable when uncle was alive so that is where this house and my jewelry are from. He had a well-paying job as a software engineer while I am just a clerk at the court. Now, I am barely managing to pay for the necessities so I would not have had any to lend to you guys. I don't know how she would know that though. Whatever it is, I would have given emotional support to your mom...Wait, hang on, did your mom call, or visit in-person?" she asks.

"Well, she doesn't have a phone, so she went in-person."

"Oh! That's why she didn't meet me because I moved to this part of town where my husband and his family live. Your grandparents and the rest of the family live further north," she takes a glance outside, "Oh, dear, it's gotten dark. Where are you supposed to be?"

"I went to tuition today and my teacher sent me out to buy mixture, but I guess I should be getting back now. I'll be on my way, bye!" I exclaim, as I am about to exit out the front door.

"Hang on, dear, I can't let you walk on your own in the dark. Let me come with you for safety. I will drop you off at your tuition teacher's home. I presume your mom is going to pick you up there," she states.

"I mean, I would have walked home by myself but since it is so late, Ma would have come there, yeah."

Raji Aunty locks up the house and packs her purse. She suddenly looks so joyful! Just a minute before, she had been dull, pondering about our life.

As we walk away from the house, I ask her, "Between you and me, you are also coming to see my mom, right?"

She winks, "Haha, you got me! What can I say? We are best friends, and it has been so long."

We keep walking and bump into these two kids

dashing through the street. They are a boy and girl, both looking to be about Kanna's age. We almost lose our balance as they play tag around our legs. The path was narrow as it is, so it was quite uncomfortable to be wobbling around near the children.

"Kids, do you mind playing outside of the walkway?" Raji Aunty asks, kindly.

Her personality exactly replicates that of an elementary school teacher. I tell her that and she laughs. She says she would love to be a teacher of any sort because she loves children and teaching them. When she gets financially stable enough, she will switch from her law clerk job to a teacher.

"Why did you choose to work as a court clerk, Aunty?" I ask.

"Dear, it wasn't really a choice. After I got married, I enjoyed a few years off from any work while Uncle was the breadwinner, but his passing was like a wake-up call for me. I realized I have to earn money to survive and eventually become independent. My friend, Lakshmi, was working at the court and as they were hiring for the clerk position, she put in my name, and I got hired. The job is quite simple. I just sit through trials and type the transcripts of what both sides say. Occasionally, I pass up evidence to the judges. This job taught me that it is a good thing that I am literate. It is what saved me and allowed me to lead a solo life. That is part of the reason I pity your mom because..." she pauses.

"Because she isn't literate?" I ask, slowly.

Raji Aunty nods, "Yes, if she knew how to read and write, she would be able to work a higher-paying job. She must be reverting to her washerwoman skills she learned from her mother. It really is unfortunate how poorly human labor is paid compared to brain power. You know, that is why western countries like America are superior in some ways because manual efforts get paid decently, what to do."

"Why didn't Ma go to school?"

"Well, based on what I have explained about your grandparents, you can tell they are very traditional-minded. They didn't believe girls needed an education. It is really sad when you think about it because I am facing the situation where a woman doesn't have a man to support herself. An education is a valuable asset for all. Besides, they could hardly pay for food and invested all their resources into farming, including your mother. She toiled on the fields when she could have been studying and building her future. She has probably told you and your brother to study, right?" she asks.

I nod, "Aunty, Ma cares deeply about our education, but we don't have the funds to pay for school."

"Wait, what? Why didn't you tell me earlier, Nikitha? Are you not going to school?"

"No, Aunty, which is actually why I am being sent to Shami Aunty's house for tuition so I can learn. She is a friend's mom who offered to tutor me for free. This is just temporary until Ma has enough money to send us to school."

"I understand, dear, but these foundational years are crucial for your education if you want to have a successful life. Your mom should prioritize sending at least you to school and slowly saving up fees for your brother. I will talk to her about this when I meet her. Is there anything major you haven't told me yet?" she asks, concerned.

"Nope, that's all, Aunty. But there is one thing I wanted to tell you about. Something I saw on the way to your house. It is still stuck in my mind, and I can't get it out."

I proceed to describe the whole incident about the cows including the poor baby calf. I explain how all of them were being neglected and looked unhealthy. I just had to get this off my chest and Raji Aunty living in that area might have an idea about it. I also mention

Abdul and his servant who were behaving very harshly towards the animals.

She ponders for a while and replies, "Nikitha, I know exactly what you are referring to. There is a cow farm on the path from the town. Over the past couple of years, it has exchanged hands multiple times. I remember the owner two years before, Hamid Uncle. He had gotten really old and became bedridden, so he passed it on to his grandson, Abdul...I have always had a soft spot for those cows. Many years ago, they were so sweet, and they used to greet villagers who walked past."

I ask, "Used to? What happened?"

"I am not exactly sure, but your mom and I used to come to this village when we were kids and people would always visit the cows. It was such a wholesome sight. They would feed the cows all sorts of fresh fruits, veggies, and grains. Everyone was happy and the entire community cared for the cows properly. Nowadays, this kind of spectacle never happens."

"Where they not used for meat then?" I ask.

"Oh, heavens, no! Back then, an old couple owned these cows. They were vegetarian just like us and cherished these cows. They shared the joy with the village. Unfortunately, after they passed away, these cows were sold to a nonvegetarian family, who converted it into a meat farm. They were the ancestors of Hamid Uncle and Abdul. Ever since then, a lot of people yearn for those old days when the cows were like 'pets' but that isn't happening again."

"What can I do to make it happen?" I ask, empowered.

"Hold your horses there, Nikitha. I admire your passion for saving the cows, but we should approach this methodically. I know it is tempting to just set them free like you were wanting to, haha, I would have done that too. But we have to think of more logical approaches. I will keep brainstorming and reach out to you if I think of something."

"Oh, yeah, that's great, thank you!" I smile at her, and she smiles back.

I know comparing people is a toxic trait, but I cannot help thinking that Raji Aunty is way better than Shami Aunty. As an aunty, teacher, and friend, she is just the full package: responsible, kind, and caring. I wish she were the one teaching me instead. I know she would never send me out on a wild goose chase for mixture like Shami Aunty did.

After a long walk, we are finally back in front of Shami Aunty's house. It looks completely different at night with the darkness making the white house look brighter. On top of that, they have fairy lights strung across the top that are flashing colors. They are highlighting a huge poster. I struggle to read it in the dark but immediately, front and center, I see the picture.

"Oh, my goodness," Raji Aunty pauses.

CHAPTER 13
PUNISHED AND PREJUDICE

I am dumbfounded by what I see. There is a giant poster, about two feet by five feet, which says "MISSING CHILD" in bold print. The lettering is in neon shades, so it is visible at night. Right beside it, there is a giant photo of none other than me.

The photo is so embarrassing as it is from when I

was little, making a funny face. I guess it was the only one they could find. And since it had to be visible at night, they made my eyes and hair neon green. I look like an alien!

It is labeled "Nikitha Krishnan, age 10". The poster, or better yet banner, has other details of where I was last seen and such, but what catches my eye the most is the prize money.

Apparently, if someone finds me, they will receive ☐10,000! That is an enormous sum of money that I have seen people bring in briefcases in movies and TV. There is no way Ma is paying this much and there is no reason for Shami Aunty to, so I wonder who is.

Meanwhile, Raji Aunty has other concerns in mind, so she asks, "Nikitha, dear, how long have you been missing?"

"I thought it was only a few hours, Aunty. What time is it?"

She checks her vintage gold watch and says, "Around 9 pm."

"Oh, then I have been gone for quite a while, like 7 hours."

"Gosh, your mom must have been worrying. We shouldn't have been talking for so long. Let's get you inside," she grabs my hand, and we walk into the house.

I brace myself for Ma's scolding and Shami Aunty's gushing. Immediately, I see Ma sitting in the front couch with Shami Aunty on the other side. They seem to be glaring at each other. I can sense the tension in the room.

Once she sees me, she runs to give me a hug, "Nikku, where were you? We have been looking around for hours."

"Shami Aunty sent me out to buy mixture but don't worry, I was with Raji Aunty the whole time."

"Raji, is that you?" Ma asks, longingly.

"Kamla!" Raji Aunty exclaims and they hug for a

long time.

"It is good you're back, Nikitha," Shami Aunty carefully states.

I can sense the tension between Ma and Shami Aunty. Ma has her jaw clenched. She is trying her best to avoid scolding her since she cannot. We poor people must always respect the rich. It is just how things work.

"Ma, let's go home so I am ready for tomorrow's class."

"Tomorrow's class? You are not coming back here. I will never jeopardize your safety again!"

"Kamla, please calm down and don't make any hasty decisions. I realize I should not have sent Nikitha to the store, and I promise this will never happen again. Please forgive me and give me another chance," Shami Aunty pleads.

I don't understand. Why is she begging so much for me to stay? She is gaining no profit from tutoring me.

Ma is one step ahead of me and asks, "What are you getting out of teaching Nikitha? Why do you want her to stay so badly?"

"Kamla, it is nothing like in the realm of what you are thinking. It is just that I enjoy teaching Nikitha, and I want to help. As I told you when we first discussed this, I don't want her to miss out on an education because of your financial difficulties. From the goodness of my heart, I want to help her learn."

"We don't need your pity. I would rather pay for actual school than risk my daughter's safety. Come on, Nikku," Ma grabs my hand.

I feel helpless. I know it will be a while before Ma can afford school and I had more fun today than all of the days I was at home. I look towards Raji Aunty who is in a corner away from screaming Ma. She looks back at me with soft eyes.

She interjects, "Kamla, Nikitha did not go far or into any dangerous situations. Please let her have this opportunity."

"Be quiet, Raji, you don't know. Let's go home, Nikku," Ma pulls me toward the door.

I sigh and take one last look at Shami Aunty's house. Near the stairs, I see Kaveer. He looks at me and sticks his tongue out. I thought the higher education at school would have taught him to be more mature, but he hasn't changed one bit. I ignore him and walk with Ma. Raji Aunty follows us out of the house she was not invited to in the first place.

Outside Shami Aunty's house, Ma is relieved to have me with her. Then, there is a moment of awkward silence between Ma and Raji Aunty. Neither of them knows what to say to the other.

"It's a coincidence that you guys are meeting after all these years, huh?" I laugh to break the ice.

"Yes, it certainly is. It is so good to see you, Kamla. I'm sorry for everything that happened. I should have been more supportive and spoke up to Mom and

Dad about Krishna."

"Don't worry about it, Raji. No matter what you could have said, they were stubborn and would never have listened...Let's leave the past in the past. It is nice to meet again. I am sorry for not calling you all these years. I know us sisters should always stick together."

Sisters, what? Ma and Raji Aunty are sisters?!

CHAPTER 14
SISTERS FOREVER

"You guys are sisters?" I ask, shocked.

"Yes, did Raji not tell you?" Ma asks, glaring at Raji Aunty who is supposedly her sister.

I shake my head and glare at Raji Aunty too. She

is under pressure to reply.

"Okay, okay, I lied. Sorry. But I didn't know what else to do," Raji Aunty spits out.

"What do you mean?" I ask.

"I didn't know how you would react if I told you I was your mom's sister. I also didn't know if your mom would want you to know. It was such a complicated situation. On top of this, your grandparents told me not to talk to you all. I had to make a quick decision on the spot. But I'm glad I met you. Sisters forever," Raji Aunty chuckles.

They hug one more time and I look away. It feels awkward to be around two grown adults hugging. Then, they realize how I am feeling and pull me into a huge group hug.

"So, Raji Aunty, you are my real aunt!" I exclaim.

After some more laughs over conversation, we notice we are still in the street in front of Shami Aunty's house. Ma graciously invites Raji Aunty home for dinner with us.

"It's okay if you can't make it or need to go home to your family, but it'll be nice for us to chat some more and you can meet my son, Kanna."

There is a moment of stone silence. Raji Aunty and I look at each other. Ma doesn't understand the pause.

Raji Aunty slowly starts, "I don't have a family, Kamla. My husband passed away."

Ma is shaken and doesn't know what to say. She always thought her situation was the worst, her husband being in jail, but Raji Aunty's is way worse.

"That's awful, Raji. Why didn't you ever reach out? I would have helped you...No, never mind, don't answer that. I know why. But don't say you don't have a family since you have us. Do you live with Mom and Dad now?" Ma asks, referring to my grandparents.

She shakes her head, "No, I am working as a clerk at the court near my husband's village, so I decided to stay in our house. And besides, Mom and Dad have not changed one bit. They are still into their old habits, and I didn't want to deal with their incessant comments, interfering with my life. They are still living happily in our old house. They insisted many times for me to move in with them or vice versa but I never budged, and they have accepted it at this point."

Ma laughs and playfully nudges Raji Aunty, "Ha, you have not changed at all. Once a rebel, always a rebel. I am so proud you're an independent woman, though! So, do you want to stay for dinner or not?"

"Thanks for the offer but not today since it is getting dark, and I should walk home before it is too late. We should keep meeting though and you guys should come over, too."

"We definitely will, bye!"

As we are almost done saying our goodbyes, I ask Raji Aunty a question that has been bugging me, "If you are sisters, then how come only *you* know how to read?"

Earlier, it made sense that their different sets of parents valued their education differently but now it doesn't make sense.

Ma looks at Raji Aunty, "Exactly how much have you told her?"

Raji Aunty raises her hands up, "Hey, hey, don't blame me. I just answered her questions. Your daughter is quite the detective, always interrogating!"

I giggle and she explains that from an early age, she was academically advanced. Both Ma and Raji Aunty attended elementary school, but all the teachers recommended Raji Aunty to continue further studies. She was interested as well so she was sent to Kashmir to live with their rich relatives. She left when they were young and only returned as a teenager.

"How were you able to afford so many years of education?" I ask, being well aware of how expensive schooling is.

"My sister got a scholarship! She was so good the

school paid for her in full," Ma exclaims, making Raji Aunty blush.

"Oh, wow, that's awesome! Didn't you miss your family?"

"Haha, there is no chance Raji missed us. She was having the time of her life in Kashmir. She learned so much. I still think she deserves a job at a higher level. There are no limits to my sister's abilities," Ma smiles.

"Ma, why didn't you study?" I ask, slowly realizing it is an awkward question for the moment.

"Well, Nikku, dear, that's what I ask myself every day. Sure, school was challenging for me since I wasn't naturally gifted like your aunt but if I had an education, I could have been far more independent like Raji. Our family state could have improved," Ma lets out an exasperated sigh.

Raji Aunty comforts her, "It's okay, Kamla. I'm here for you. Since we are connected now, we can always lean on each other for support. Stay strong."

In that moment, I know what they are going to say so I chime in.

We all say, "Sisters forever!"

CHAPTER 15
IT'S A HARD NO!

Ma and I continue on the route home. We remain silent the entire way. The happiness of my returning has faded away and now, it is just a normal walk at night. All the shops are slowly shutting down with people outside them, talking and talking. There are lights everywhere and the mood is quite festive. I remember Abdul mentioning Eid is coming up, so everyone is feeling the celebratory vibes.

I occupy myself with thinking about how I can convince my mom to allow me to attend Shami Aunty's classes again. Although today was very chaotic, it was fun too.

I don't like to admit it to Ma but walking around everyday can be boring. I would do anything to be able to go to real school again. I love learning and being able to understand new concepts. Unlike most children, I always went to school to learn. Others would go for friends, recess, or even lunch when all I cared about were the classes.

I decide to divert the conversation and ask, "Where is Kanna?"

Talking about my brother just lights Ma up. After Pa was arrested, his birth was the first positive event. She just cajoles him so much and even though he is three, she still treats him like a newborn baby. She always calls him "my little baby". He was her comfort for the past few years and has kept her busy.

Sometimes I do feel jealous that he is loved so much but he has never known his father and that has got to hurt badly. It is sad because even Pa was excited for a new baby to be born but fate got in the way preventing them from meeting. I just hope that we will be able to free him at least for Kanna's sake.

"He is staying at Arithjai's house. I decided to leave him there since I didn't expect picking you up to take this long. Hopefully it is not disturbing their family. Let's quickly pick him up on the way."

If there is anyone my brother loves more than myself and my mom, it is Arithjai. They are practically like family and want to spend all their time together. I know at three years old, all children are friendly with each other, but these two are different. They have known each other since nursery.

Arithjai's parents, Mirali Aunty and Narinder Uncle, are good people. They regularly feed the poor people at the temple. They are not that much richer than us but have a heart of gold and want to share their wealth with charity.

When we pick up Kanna, he seems so joyous to see me and hugs me, squealing, "Nikku, Nikku, you're back!"

I hug him back but feel embarrassed as everyone on the street is looking at us because of his loud voice.

As I mentioned, Arithjai's parents are always so generous. Even at 10 pm at night when they are getting ready to sleep, they offer to make us dinner but Ma kindly refuses. She says she already has dinner ready at home but we both know that isn't true.

We go back to our hut and eat the lentils and rice

in my tiffin box I forgot to bring. I explain how Shami aunty forced me to stay and eat there. Ma was too exhausted to ask any follow-up questions but remembers to add that it shouldn't be a problem anymore since I am no longer going. Ugh, I was hoping she would rethink it. What should I tell her?

"Ma, can I please go for one more day? I promise I will stay in their house and focus on learning. Please, please, please!" I beg.

She sternly shakes her head, "No way am I letting you go back there! Shami Aunty literally endangered you by telling you to get her mixture. She could have easily gotten it herself or better yet, with a servant, but instead she sends you. How dare she?!"

She is fuming so I try to calm her down, "Ma, it's okay. If you really want me to stay home, I will."

I made that decision from my head to make my mom happy. After everything we have gone through and the battles she has fought for us, the thought of making her panic is not something I can bear.

Still, my heart wants to go back to Shami Aunty's house tomorrow. I know she might have mixed feelings about teaching me when my mom doesn't want it, but I want to at least talk to her.

Apparently, my face is showing my confusion and dismay that Ma looks at me, pitifully, "I'm sorry, Nikku. It's for your own good...hey, this could lead to something better. Tomorrow, you can go around the town at your leisure. It will be fun!"

I decide to smile to make Ma satisfied. Like I said, I would do anything for her. As I lie down, I hear the snores of Ma and Kanna. I feel satisfied that they are able to rest. I can't say the same for myself, though, because I contemplate until the wee hours of the night, coming up with ideas on what to do about the Shami Aunty situation.

CHAPTER 16
THE GREAT SNEAK-IN

At the crack of dawn, I rise with a big, gleaming

smile. I figured out what I am going to do! Ma may have

banned me from going to Shami Aunty's classes but that doesn't mean I can't visit her house. I am still allowed to roam so I will just go on a long walk near her house and pop inside.

I silently exit the hut, careful not to wake Ma and Kanna, and dash through the village. It is not long before I am in front of Shami Aunty's palace. I had this all thought out but still, the last-minute jitters get me.

THUMP-THUMP, THUMP-THUMP! My heart is racing. I can't believe I'm about to do this. I realize the only person I am hiding from is Ma and there is no way she is going to come around here. The mission plan is to go in, talk to Shami Aunty, and return to roaming.

I walk towards the entrance and the bodyguard takes one glance at me. He opens the door without question. He probably doesn't know about the drama that went down last night and assumes that I am just returning for another day of "school".

I walk inside and the house is oddly quiet. I

decide to go upstairs to find Shami Aunty since that is where she was yesterday.

As I walk up the stairs, I see it is lined with family photos which I hadn't noticed yesterday. I see pictures of Shami Aunty and Srikanth Uncle's wedding, young Shami Aunty, and baby Kaveer. They all look so different and happier in those photos. There is a glimmer in their eyes that has disappeared altogether now. They also lived a simpler life back then. Shami Aunty wore simple kurtis instead of the neon clothing she wears now. Ma has told me that the more money people earn, the greedier and more unhappy they get. Maybe it is true.

When I get to the top of the flight of stairs, I see the open area with four room doors around it. Shami Aunty is nowhere to be seen, in fact, there are no people around. I had only been shown my "school" room on the left, but I see one of the doors on the right is slightly open. I debate on whether I should go in or not.

I carefully peep open the door, ensuring I don't make any noise, and see a breathtaking sight. The walls are painted a beautiful shade of sage green and covered in posters of animals and snippets of National Geographic articles. The print on the walls is banana leaves like in the jungle.

I am awestruck by the photography of baby animals on the far wall, each with a matching hyper-realistic drawing. The artwork is so similar to the photos that one cannot tell the difference if not for the labels.

Each animals' eyes are so captivating. The one that specifically captures my heart is the baby white Harp seal with the deepest black eyes. I investigate them and see a glimpse of his soul. It just makes me sympathize even more with his rescue story from a wildlife rescue listed on the side.

It says that when he was a pup, he was found beached on the Canadian shore and a group of kind rescuers, brought him to the nearby veterinarian to be treated. Poor thing accidentally swallowed a piece of plastic and choked on it.

This makes me feel so bad but kind of lucky since our village does not use a lot of plastic. Because of our customs and traditions, we mainly use cloth and fabric. We have never considered using more sophisticated materials like paper and plastic. Without knowing it, we are a sustainable community. It's kind of ironic. If only the rest of the world would learn from us.

I am confused about whose rain forest themed room I am in until I see the "KAVEER" sign right in the middle of it. Oh, shoot, I accidentally stepped into my enemy's bedroom! I hurry toward the door so I can leave quickly but I stop right there, dead in my tracks.

Near the doorframe, I see Kaveer in his pajama shirt and shorts.

He yawns and asks, angrily, "What are you doing back here, Nikitha?! I thought my mom told you off yesterday!"

I sigh and explain, "Kaveer, I just came to talk to her and for the record, it was *my* mom who wanted to pull me out of classes. Your mom loves me and would never kick me out!"

"I wouldn't be too sure about that. Mom is nice to everyone and you're nothing special. Anyway, why are you here so early?" he asks.

I hate how he always wants to say mean things to me. Ma has told me that some people are just like that and there is nothing we can do to change them. We just have to ignore them and move on with life. It is like that famous saying that you cannot get rid of all the thorns, but you can wear shoes to protect your feet. Rather than becoming angry or trying to correct Kaveer's behavior, I take a deep breath and calm myself.

"Okay, okay, I don't know if your mom likes me or not, but I certainly think she is a nice person. I want to explain to her what happened and figure out a work around for us."

"Alrighty, then," he groans, "Good luck with that."

There is a moment of awkward silence.

I start, "Those animal drawings and photographs are so cool! Did you make them?"

He cautiously nods his head and states, "I drew them based on the pictures I took."

I exclaim in joy, "That's awesome! How come you never told us about your art in school? You must share your artistic skills!"

I realize I have startled him, so I apologize but am still eagerly awaiting a response.

"Nikitha, you're not going to understand. Just leave it, okay?"

"No, there is no way I am going to leave it! Tell me why you are hiding this part of you."

"Because...because...boys are not supposed to be good at art!" he spits out.

CHAPTER 17
CLIMATE PROBLEMS

I am shocked and don't know what to say.

Kaveer's face immediately droops, and it looks like he is

about to cry. He walks over to the bed and slumps down, holding his face in his hands. I go sit next to him, comforting him.

"It's okay, Kaveer. There is no such thing as girls' and boys' things. Those are just stupid stereotypes in society! As you know I play jacks with my neighborhood boys. At first, they looked at me weirdly for being the only girl in the group but now they eagerly welcome me and call me from my house. Who decided that jacks or in your case, art, is for a specific gender?" I ask.

He sighs, "I don't know but my friends used to tease me about my drawing a lot. It made me feel ashamed about it and that's why I don't tell anyone. I'm not hiding it on purpose, but I have no choice."

"I get it, but try to be prouder of it...Do you like animals too?" I ask, pointing at the animal posters and drawings.

He laughs, "Yeah, I love them especially wild animals. I think they are fascinating and feel bad for them as well. Climate change and global warming are deeply affecting their lives and that it is unfair!"

"Climate change? Global warming? What are those?"

"You don't know what those are?! Practically everyone nowadays is aware of those crises. This school year, in fifth grade, our curriculum focuses on those pressing issues. Basically, in simple terms, global warming is when the Earth is getting hotter now causing problems like icebergs melting, sea levels rising, wildfires, and more. Climate change is another way to describe why global warming is happening."

"How do you know so much?" I ask, astonished as Kaveer was never so intellectual before.

"Well, my teacher told me to join the Climate Change club this year and this is all we discuss about."

"Wow, there were never clubs when I was in school! A lot has changed."

"Actually, this is not at the school we used to go

to. This school year, Mom and Dad switched me to the new private school that opened in town. They invest a lot more funds in student extracurricular activities like clubs and competitions. Every student is required to take part in at least two clubs. I am in Climate Change club and Math club."

"Oh, I see. I understand that climate change is a serious problem. Why hasn't anyone solved it? What can we do to solve it?" I ask.

"Nikitha, slow your roll there. It is not easy to solve global warming. It is caused by the environment which is not in our control. People are definitely trying to improve climate change by reducing the emission of fossil fuels, but it is not quick and will take a long time! There are trivial things we can do like recycling and reducing food waste, but your enthusiasm is great."

I smile and say, "Thanks. I am just surprised since I have never heard of it...Hey, wait, do you know anything about animal rights?"

"Of course I do! Animal rights are my favorite cause since I love to help animals live better lives. Why do you ask?"

I carefully narrate the story of the poor cows to him. With every detail of their neglect, he reacts in shock.

At the end, he cries, "Oh gosh, that is horrible! We have to do something! But, what to do, is the question..."

We start discussing ideas, beginning from the craziest possibilities to the most probable. Like that we could call eccentric detectives to create a case on Abdul or that we could set up a cow buffet for them ourselves to eat their favorite foods. It was difficult to come up with an idea that was realistic yet would not get us caught.

I tell him that my first instinct was to simply open the gate and set them free.

To that, he warns, "No, no, you should never do

that! These cows were probably domestically raised so they won't know how to fend for themselves in the wild. At this point, I think the best thing for us is to seek legal help. Do you know any lawyers or people that work at the court?"

As I am about to reply, we hear loud, thunderous footsteps outside his door.

"Hide!" he whispers.

CHAPTER 18
BRAINSTORM

I hurry to hide underneath Kaveer's bed. I suck in my breath and hold it in for as long as I can.

I hear a groggy voice from outside, calling,

"Kaveer, are you awake, son? Get ready, quickly!"

I glance up at the room clock and see it is 8 am already! School starts at 8:30 am sharp so Kaveer must be fast to avoid being late. Being late for school is the worst possible thing you can do. The teachers hate it. They will give you a nasty stink-eye and make an embarrassing comment, causing the whole class to erupt in laughter. I don't know what it is like at his private school, but it is better to be safe than sorry. Kaveer looks up the same time I do, and I can see the panic in his face.

"Yes, Mom, I will get ready right now!" he calls back.

Shami Aunty opens the door and looks around the room and back at Kaveer. I stay as hidden as I can underneath the bad. She immediately stares at the gigantic pile of crumbled up pieces of paper from our early-morning brainstorming session.

"What is this?" she asks, pointing to the pile.

"Nothing...I mean, this morning I was just thinking about what to write for our school's...uh...short story competition. These are drafts of my ideas," he lies.

Shami Aunty sighs and takes that measly excuse for the truth. She reminds him once again to get ready quickly and leaves the room. When the coast is clear, Kaveer tells me to come out.

"Wow, I didn't realize the time was going so quickly. I'll just shower and get dressed. What do *you* want to do?" he asks, hesitantly.

"There is something I wanted to tell you. You asked if I know anyone working at the court and I do, actually. My aunt, Raji Aunty, is a clerk there. I told her about this cow story too and she was interested in helping."

"Wait, is she the lady who was with you yesterday?" he asks.

I nod, "Yes, she is compassionate and would definitely want to help. The only problem is that if I want to contact her, I will need to do it through Ma."

"Your mom doesn't know about this, does she?"

I hesitate and answer, "Nope. And I know she is not going to like it one bit."

"Wait a second, why do you need to contact her through your mom? Don't you know where your aunt lives?"

That is such a smart idea, so I reply, "Yes, I do! I don't know why I didn't consider it. We could go straight to my aunt's house together."

"Yeah, but remember, I have school today. Your aunt is probably also working today. How about you meet me at school when it ends, and we can walk over there together?"

"Deal! But won't your mom get worried if you don't come home on time?"

"True...I'll just tell her I'm going to hang out with some friends after school. We will need to go to your aunt's house and get back as soon as we can...Well, I got to go now, bye!" he exclaims and dashes out of the room.

My first thought is that I have to leave Kaveer's room as soon as I can. If someone sees me, I'm toast. I look around the room to analyze my options.

There is the most obvious choice: getting out the same way I came from, through the front door. But that wouldn't work since someone would see me for sure; if it's not Kaveer's parents, it would be a servant. I can't run the risk of them seeing me and calling Ma. She would be furious that I ran off here. That just leaves two options: climbing out the window or just waiting for the coast to be clear.

I realize it is not logical for me to wait that long and I can never be completely sure it is safe so I should just climb out the window. It is a large glass window with gold metal surrounding it. I gently slide it open wide enough for me to fit in. I jump up onto the windowsill and look outside to see the view.

The window is right above a part of the roof which slides down close to the ground. I sit on the roof and gently maneuver myself downwards. Eventually I am a few feet off the ground, so I jump down. When I land on my feet, I run over to the gate and exit. I feel relieved as I leave the property, unseen and unheard.

CHAPTER 19
AFTER-SCHOOL

On my way home, my tummy is turning, and I almost feel sick. I have to find some way to pass the time until Kaveer's school ends at 3 pm. It is only 9 am, so I still have six long hours!

I decide to head straight to the market since it is Tuesday, and they always have great things there on Tuesdays. My favorite are the lychees! They are juicy, white fruits that taste like jelly. Tara Aunty sells them fresh from her family's farm.

Back when Pa was around, he would take me there in the summertime and buy me a few lychees every week.

Ma would scold him since she believed as we are running low on money for the necessities itself, he should not be spoiling me by buying exotic fruits.

He would chuckle, "Don't worry about it, Kamla. Nikku should enjoy her childhood and lychees are worth it!"

I look around and a lot has changed at the market since the last time I went there a few years ago. The original vendors have been replaced by businesses. That is what usually happens to these kinds of places –

the small vendors can't keep up with the large-scale businesses who buy them.

I keep walking, looking at the stalls which range from fruits and vegetables to cotton purses. Eventually, I walk into a new section: meat.

My instinct tells me to turn back and not look at meat. Instead, I decide to just see what there is. I see aisles of shrimp, fish, and chicken.

Eventually, there it is. I am shocked to see the last stall on the line is "Abdul's Beef". On the table, there are pieces of red meat laid out. I am disgusted by the sight since I have never seen raw meat let alone beef.

I have a strong feeling it is the same guy, Abdul, and sure enough, there is his assistant. The man is talking to another guy in whispers. They are discussing how there are few sales today.

One guy says, "Bro, don't worry about that, we're getting in more cow meat from Abdul sir's farm next week when the cows are fat enough."

"Oh, great then the fresh flesh should attract more customers!"

They both cackle in unison the same way Abdul did. Maybe everyone who works at the farm is trained to cackle identically. It would be cool yet creepy if that were the case.

They are completely wrong, though, as even if the meat had more flesh, they would still not have any customers. Any person with even an ounce of common sense would know the real reason they don't have any customers is because hardly enough in this town eats meat. I don't know what Abdul is trying to do, selling meat to a community of vegetarians.

I am horrified by the fact that those poor cows, including Soniya, will be slaughtered next week. I run as fast as I can to Kaveer's school building and wait outside for the rest of the time.

I am utterly bored but there is nothing better to

do and I have had enough wandering. I observe the school all the rich kids go to. It is quite different from the school I went to, where any kid that isn't rich goes. All kids in our area had to go there because it was the only school before this private school opened.

Kaveer's school is a private school which costs a boatload of money to attend. He attended the same school as me until fourth grade but then switched this year for fifth grade when the private school opened.

Finally, after what seems like an eternity, the bell rings three times signifying that school is over! All the kids run out of the school building in matching uniforms, with their backpacks on their backs and holding their lunch bags.

I didn't realize that having to see my former classmates again would be such an awkward interaction. Random girls who would gossip about me and guys who would tease me just stare in awe.

I assumed most people knew what happened

with Pa and why Ma had to withdraw me from school, but I guess not.

Randomly, a popular girl, Parvi yells, "Nikitha, is that really you? Girl, we thought you had literally vanished. Haha, it is so *not* good to see you."

She laughs hysterically and her entourage joins her. They look and sound like a pack of hyenas, laughing their heads off. I glare at them but before I can say something snarky back, I spot Kaveer amongst his group of boys. They are all laughing and joking around. When he spots me, he says bye to the boys and walks over.

"Wow, you're right on time," he smiles.

As we walk further into the street, I tell him, "Yep. I was waiting all day for this."

Then, I fill him in on what I saw at the market. His face shows how disgusted he is.

"That means we only have a week to save these cows. We better get to work!" he exclaims.

I lead him to Raji Aunty's village. We decide to see her first and decide the next steps before visiting the cows. Maybe we could all go together to assess the situation. After a lot of walking and hearing Kaveer complaining that it is too far, we reach her house. We walk to the door, and I knock.

"Coming!" someone yells from the inside.

Raji Aunty quickly opens the door, and she is surprised to see me.

"Nikku! It is so good to see you. This is kind of funny," she laughs.

"Why?" I ask.

"Because I'm here," someone says from behind her.

Raji Aunty moves over and there, I see Ma with Kanna behind her. I am so shocked. What are they doing here? I immediately ask her that, but she takes it the wrong way.

"I should be asking you that! What are you doing

here and with...Shami's son?" she asks, looking over at Kaveer.

"We wanted Raji Aunty's help with something and it's kind of complicated. I'll explain inside."

We both walk in while Ma is glaring at us the whole way. I never would have thought she would come here in the middle of work. We all sit around the table and Ma tells me to reveal everything. I carefully narrate the cow story for her even though Kaveer and Raji Aunty had already heard it.

When I am done, Ma asks, "So, you really want to save those cows, huh?"

Kaveer and I nod together.

"Well, get that thought out of your minds!" she screams.

CHAPTER 20
LAWYER IN THE HOUSE

Everyone in the room stares at Ma including Raji Aunty. Kaveer is especially surprised at her response because he is not used to her sudden angry outbursts.

"I'm sorry, but I don't want you to get involved in

activism for problems you find in the community. Only focus on your own lives. That's how you can avoid getting in trouble."

"Ma, but it's really important. Those poor cows are going to be slaughtered next week. The baby will *never* have a chance to see life. We need to save them!" I cry.

"Yes, Aunty, please allow us. We promise to be careful. We actually came here to get Raji Aunty's help on this mission. We won't do anything unsupervised," Kaveer adds.

Ma sighs and agrees, "Fine, but don't take any risks and always listen to Raji Aunty."

Immediately, we thank her, and she leaves back to the river to wash clothes, bringing Kanna with her. It is just Raji Aunty, Kaveer, and I left.

"This latest information you found at the market is serious news. We must act quickly to save these cows. What did you guys need help with?" Raji Aunty asks.

"We thought seeking legal help would be the safest option. Nikitha mentioned you work at the court so we were wondering if you could connect us to a lawyer," Kaveer replies, confidently.

Wow, he took the words right out of my mouth. He would be a great businessman since he knows how to speak his mind.

"Ah, I see. Well, I guess today's your lucky day! In about fifteen minutes, one of my lawyer friends is going to come here. Once Nikku told me about these cows, I went to work the next day and started talking to her. She is an animal rights lawyer and would be perfect for the job!" Raji Aunty exclaims.

We are surprised and thank her, repeatedly. Raji Aunty truly is the best!

A few minutes later, someone knocks on the door. Raji Aunty opens it, and we see a quaint little woman in a business suit.

"Raji!" she exclaims, and they both hug it out.

Raji Aunty introduces her, "This is Sejal, an animal rights lawyer at our court. I have already talked to her about the cow case, and she is willing to take it up for free as a service to you children."

We introduce ourselves and thank her for her time and generosity. She seems super bubbly and enthusiastic. Eventually, we all decide to head to the "sight" as Sejal Aunty calls it to see what we have to work with.

We go on the long walk there, occasionally having some small talk between ourselves. It is mostly the aunties and the kids having separate conversations, though. Finally, we reach the cow shed. It is later in the evening so most of the cows are on the floor resting. I notice Soniya, the sick calf I saw last time, seems to be doing much better. I am glad.

At once, Sejal Aunty shrieks, "This is unbelievable! There is not even enough space for them all to lie down at once. It must be a nightmare for the ones who have to sleep standing up. This is completely unacceptable. And which calf were you concerned about, Nikitha?"

"That one," I say, pointing to the golden Soniya, "She was really sick the last time I saw her a week ago, but luckily, I think she has improved a lot now. I'm less worried about her and more concerned about saving all of them."

"Alright then, me too. I just need to take some photographs and notes as evidence upon seeing the scene. I will go home and have all these typed up in a report and will get a trial scheduled in the next few days. Abdul's company will get summoned to the court and they will have their lawyer fight. Don't worry, though, your Sejal Aunty will not let you down. We will win!" she laughs.

"That's great, Aunty, but please make sure the trial is as soon as possible. We can't risk having them change their mind and slaughter the animals early,"

Kaveer replies, worried.

She assures us that everything will be okay, and I tell them about how I entered the cage the other day to comfort Soniya and that I named the calf.

Raji Aunty is shocked, "Nikku, that's dangerous! What if they attack?"

I look at the cows and notice they have become fatter and stronger. Hopefully, Abdul's men didn't force-feed them. But I still trust they won't harm us. I tell her this and following my lead, the three of them enter the cage with me.

We all go to our favorite cows and sit by them. Soniya is always my favorite, so I sit next to her and continue petting her. She looks up at me as if she remembers me; no one will know if she really does but the thought feels nice.

After we are done, we lock the gate and agree to meet at the court for the trial. We go our separate ways: Kaveer and I walk towards our town, Raji Aunty goes back to her village, and Sejal Aunty goes to wherever she lives. Now it is just a waiting game until the trial.

CHAPTER 21
THE TRIAL

HIT-HIT-HIT! The judge bangs his gavel on the table to start the trial. In just a few days after our last meeting, Sejal Aunty had a trial set up and Raji Aunty told me when I visited her house.

Before the trial, we had to collect signatures from our parents allowing us to be there without their supervision. Ma was hesitant since she felt a child going to the courthouse is dangerous. She had bad memories from Pa's many trials, so she was even more apprehensive. With a lot of convincing from Sejal Aunty and Raji Aunty that I am an eyewitness so I must be there, she agreed and signed the form.

Shami Aunty on the other hand was awestruck when we told her. She did not hear about anything related to the cow rescue mission until right before the trial. We then realized that it was during Kaveer's school day. His mom was not okay with him missing school and to be honest, there was no need for him to be there as he wasn't even an eyewitness.

Now, in the courtroom, the judge, Judge Davis, begins with some formalities. The clerks read out the name of the case and the parties involved. I am on the plaintiff side with Sejal Aunty and Raji Aunty. For once,

Raji Aunty has taken a day off from her job as a clerk to be with us.

On the defendant side, I see Abdul with his men and a lawyer. The lawyer looks exhausted and like he does not want to be there. Knowing Abdul, he probably paid him a hefty amount to argue for them in the trial. Although I don't think they will win as *we* have the law on our side.

Sejal Aunty starts by arguing why *Abdul's Beef Farm* is a place of animal neglect and abuse. She submits the photographs and notes she took to the judge who takes a look at them and responds with his mouth wide open to the gruesome sight.

After, Abdul whispers in his lawyer's ear who stands up and starts speaking.

"Your honor, the company, *Abdul's Beef Farm*, has all the proper licensing and registration for a meat-raising and slaughtering facility. It is a completely legal farm," he says.

That is such a weak argument, but we expected they would use it as it is basically all they have. Sejal Aunty immediately bites back with her extensive points about how it qualifies as animal neglect. Just by listening to her arguments, you can tell that she is an experienced animal rights lawyer who knows what she is doing. She describes how they are not given nutritious food and clean water which is a requirement to all animals. Cows are especially supposed to be allowed to graze, and the sick cows must be tended to. She goes on and on and with every point she brings up, we notice Abdul and his team's hearts sinking.

Our group's goal was to not have the cows killed but after some searching, we found that it is completely legal to kill animals for business. That is why we approached the case as an animal neglect problem so we would have them release the cows and then ensure they are not killed when they are free.

Abdul whispers in his lawyer's ear again who gets

up and asks, "Do you have any eyewitnesses?"

"Yes, we do," Sejal Aunty grabs my hand, and we stand up, "This is Nikitha Krishnan. She was the one who first observed the animal abuse at *Abdul's Beef Farm* and is our side's eyewitness. Your honor, may we have your permission to have Nikitha speak?"

"A child?! That's absurd. Your honor, you cannot allow a child to be an eyewitness!" Abdul yells, showing how he did not expect us to have an eyewitness at all.

"Silence! Do not talk back to me, mister. If you are not an advocate, you must get permission to speak. It is quite unusual for a child to be an eyewitness but let us hear what Nikitha has to see. Please come up, dear," the judge requests.

I am *terrified* to go up onto the podium in front of everyone and speak. We rehearsed this multiple times at home with Raji Aunty and Sejal Aunty, but I am still nervous. Public speaking is not my thing. I tremble with fear when both the aunties hug me and tell me it will be okay.

Finally, I gather the courage to walk up to the podium. The clerk brings a religious book and asks me to make the promise. I have seen this in shows before, so I know what to say.

"I promise that I will only speak the truth, the whole truth, and nothing but the truth," I say, confidently.

CHAPTER 22
MY TIME TO SPEAK

"Miss Nikitha Krishnan, please tell us in your own words what you saw at *Abdul's Beef Farm*," the judge says.

"Okay. Last week, I was walking and came across

the meat farm. There were about forty cows packed into a tiny enclosure. It was filthy since their waste was not being removed and their enclosure was not being cleaned. Their food and water containers were dirty with dry grass. Many of the cows showed signs of lethargy and illness but were not receiving medical treatment. In fact, one calf could barely stand up. She has gotten better more recently but her sickness may have lasting effects. In fact, there is not even enough space in the enclosure for all the cows to lay down at the same time so some may be suffering as they sleep standing up. This is unfair treatment to these animals."

I go on to describe more of what I see and even say that I witnessed Abdul and his men force-feeding the cows and acting hostile towards them.

"Is this true?" the judge asks Abdul.

"Judge sir, uh," Abdul hesitates.

"I asked you a question. You must answer it. Is this true?!" the judge repeats, louder.

Abdul slowly nods, "Yes, it is, but only to fatten them up. No one will buy them if they are not plump by Eid."

"Oh, I see. So, are you saying it is okay to force-feed animals if it is just to "fatten them up?""

After a few moments of awkward silence, Abdul's lawyer asks, "Your honor, I have a question for Miss Nikitha Krishnan."

I gulp in fear. Even though this lawyer does not have skill and is just a puppet saying what Abdul wants him to, I am still scared to be put on the spot. I decide to take a deep breath and see what he has to ask. The judge grants him permission and he starts the interrogation.

"So, miss, you are saying it is not okay to kill cows, but it is okay to kill other animals like chickens and goats?"

"No, not at all. I never specifically said it is not okay to kill cows but rather personally, we believe no animals should be killed but according to the law, they may if the company is licensed. Our main issue is that these cows should not live in such poor conditions. It is simply not fair to them," I state.

"Okay, then what do you think is fair to them, Nikitha?" the judge asks.

"Your honor, I believe they should be kept in a sanctuary where the villagers can care for them like they did years ago. They would not be raised for slaughter but rather as "pets." It would be a heartwarming community tradition where people could take turns feeding, cleaning, and caring for the cows. The families who are interested in playing a bigger role would be able to adopt a cow of their own. This way they can break out of poverty by having a source of income, a milk-producing cow. This would improve the state of our village. I hate to ruin Abdul uncle's business so once he makes his farm more hygienic and healthier for the animals, he can adopt some of our cows back."

The judge smiles, "You have really thought this

through. Consider it done. Clerk, please note that the outcome of this trial is to rehome the cows to a new sanctuary. This initiative will be led by Nikitha and her friends."

I smile back and bow down at the judge, "Thank you, your honor."

Abdul yells in anger and some security guards escort him outside. He frowns at me as he is being dragged out. I feel kind of bad that I ruined his source of income, but quickly realize that it involved slaughter which is horrible. I am ecstatic to have saved the cows!

HIT-HIT-HIT! The gavel ends the case. I walk over to the benches and the aunties wrap me in a big hug. They tell me I spoke with such conviction and did so well. I am so proud of myself too. I would have never thought I could do it before now.

We walk outside the courtroom, and someone wraps me in a hug from behind. I look backward to see that it is Ma with Kanna.

"Wow, Nikku, that was amazing, my dear. I loved your words out there."

I feel even happier to have made Ma happy. We all walk together to Kaveer's house to tell him the big news and celebrate our accomplishments.

CHAPTER 23
OUR NEW LIFE

That court case brought about so many positive changes to our lives. The cows were released even though Abdul argued a lot against it. We had media support which forced him to accept it. The sanctuary was in an area of lush green land which was donated by a retired farmer for this cause. Moving companies also volunteered their time to help move the cows and construction workers helped build the new fencing. The cows' new pasture was so large that each cow practically had a room to itself. They could walk around for days and eat so much delicious grass, or at least delicious for them. Volunteers cared for the cows on a daily basis. The community pitched in to make it happen.

Media people were recording my speech at the trial and released it on social media. They titled it "Village girl in India speaks up against cows in court and saves them". It went viral and many people around the world reached out. They wanted to know more about me. Once people heard about our story with Pa being accidentally arrested causing us to not have enough money for school, they were touched and donated online. It gave Ma enough money to enroll Kanna and me back into school. The lawyers heard about it and as a favor, they helped bail Pa out.

The day Pa came home was the best day of my life.

He suddenly came into the hut and said, "Hi, have you guys missed me?"

I ran up to him and jumped into his arms. He embraced me in a long hug, and he laughed his deep Santa Claus laugh. He had not changed one bit. He then introduced himself to Kanna. At first, things were awkward between them but eventually, they both became close.

In fact, the first day he came, he asked Ma, "What is the new baby's name?"

After she told him it is Kanna, he wrapped her in a big hug and said, "You remembered."

They later explained that before he left, they were thinking of baby names, and he suggested Kanna if it is a boy baby since it is another name for Lord Krishna like Pa's name. Ma remembered that and named Kanna it when he was born.

The happiest person when Pa returned was Ma.

She immediately apologized, "Sorry, Krishna, I will never scold you again. I love you, I love you, I love you!"

She turned into a different person around Pa and always giggled. They would joke around like little kids. It was fun to see them be childish!

The best part of this whole ordeal was that some of the cows at the cow farm were available for adoption. After Pa came back, we convinced Ma to adopt one. Since she grew up on a farm, she had experience caring for cows. From all the cows, you can probably guess which one I chose to adopt. That's right, we adopted Soniya. After being released to the pasture in the sanctuary, she was happier than ever and super active, always running around and playing.

We received enough donations online to build a bigger house with a backyard where Soniya lived. All of us would pitch in and care for her. I loved having my cow friend live with us. She became like a sister.

Speaking of sisters, Ma and Raji Aunty went back to being two peas in a pod and spent all their time together. When Pa met Raji Aunty, they talked for a long time. After hearing all the news, both sets of my grandparents agreed to meet us.

That was probably the most difficult meeting since it had been so long. Kanna and I had never even seen our grandparents. My parents were unsure about it but when we all met up, everything became okay.

It was just a party of hugs all around and apologies everywhere. My grandparents apologized for not being supportive and disowning my parents. They promised they would make up for the lost time by always being there with us.

I loved my grandmas because they would always feed me homemade sweets and I loved my grandpas because they would play games with us. It was such a fun time those couple weeks they stayed with us. Later,

Ma's parents moved in with Raji Aunty as she lived alone while Pa's parents lived with us.

Pa returned to his old job but was promoted to a senior civil engineer position. Ma was worried that they would not hire people who were formerly in prison but as this was all a mistake, his time in jail was erased from his permanent record.

Ma no longer needed to strain herself as a washerwoman because we sold Soniya's milk at the market and made money through that. Ma's only job was to take care of and milk Soniya every day. It was a much more relaxing job where Ma could take her long-needed rest.

Kaveer and I became friends after freeing the cows. He comes over to our house and I go over to his all the time. He is actually a great friend, and we have lots to bond over regarding animal rights and climate change. They may be unusual topics for children to talk about, but it works for us.

Ma always says you won't know the value of something until it is gone. I only understood Pa's value after he was arrested, and we couldn't spend time with him. After he returned, I cherish every moment we have together because no one knows what will happen tomorrow. Our favorite pastime is hearing his stories from jail. They are hilarious and sometimes unrealistic! No one knows if they really happened or not, I guess.

In return, we tell him about what happened in our lives - not nearly as interesting though. He is still surprised that his daughter, me, spoke in court and saved so many cows. He is filled with pride that my actions did so much.

One night, when we were lounging in the chairs, Pa asked me, "Nikku, you know something?"

"Yeah, Pa?"

"You asked if I was ever worried about getting out of jail, right? Well, I didn't need to because I always had faith that you would save me. You are truly a savior,

Nikitha. I love you."

I was so shocked I didn't know what to say. My father believed that I could bail him out before even I believed in myself. He always knew I had courage, power, and talent. I was always wondering if someday a miracle would come to save us but now, I realize that I was that miracle.

We all need those people in our lives who will trust us and help us see the light even when we can't. We all need people like Pa to guide us on the path to success.

"I love you too, Pa."

ABOUT THE AUTHOR

Akchara Mukunthu, the author of *Cows*, is a 10th grader in high school who absolutely loves to write! Previously, she has published another middle grade novel, *Miss Einstein*, on Amazon and an episode-based story, *Seen*, on Kindle Vella. She publishes articles on Medium (akchara.md) regarding animal rights issues similar to *Cows*. Besides writing, she enjoys singing, watching movies, spending time with her family and friends, and interacting with animals. She is proud to have written this book and hopes it promotes change in animal rights, especially addressing meat farms in rural towns.

Made in the USA
Columbia, SC
25 September 2024

42367005R00129